James
Jan '90

THE
COMFORTS
OF
MADNESS

THE COMFORTS OF MADNESS

PAUL SAYER

Doubleday

NEW YORK LONDON TORONTO SYDNEY AUCKLAND

PUBLISHED BY DOUBLEDAY

A division of Bantam Doubleday Dell Publishing Group, Inc.
666 Fifth Avenue, New York, New York 10103

DOUBLEDAY and the portrayal of an anchor with a dolphin
are trademarks of Doubleday, a division of Bantam Doubleday
Dell Publishing Group, Inc.

This book was originally published in Great Britain
by Constable and Company Limited in 1988. The
Doubleday edition is published by arrangement with
Constable and Company Limited.

Library of Congress Cataloging-in-Publication Data

Sayer, Paul.
     The comforts of madness / Paul Sayer. — 1st
Doubleday ed.
          p.   cm.
     ISBN 0-385-26777-0
     I. Title.
PR6069.A98C66   1990   89-37437
823'.914—dc20   CIP
                                    AC

TO ANNE AND SIMON

ONE

I HAD HOPED to remain unturned, but it was not to be.

The night nurse came with the first ashes of dawn, ripping back the bedcovers, sighing audibly, then tossing back the counterpane while he went in search of clean linen. I had fouled the bed, but it would not be much; I did not shit much, was never one for it, a smear on the pad, a marble on the drawsheet, nothing more. The heavy, young man returned saying, "Come on, out of it." He reexposed my nakedness, cupped one hand behind my neck and with his other gripped one of my rigid, crossed forearms to pull me up into a sitting position at the side of the bed. By clamping my head under his arm he was able to rustle up the drawsheet behind me and position the clean one across more than half the mattress. He picked up my legs, forcing me onto my back, then heaved me over the hillock of wet cloth, leaving me lying on my other side. He whipped the wet linen onto the floor, made one frustrated effort at trying to straighten my legs which had a habit of contracting up beneath me when I was in bed, before neatly replacing the sheet, blanket, and counterpane and returning about his weary business of checking the rest of the patients in the dormitory.

None of this was particularly remarkable; it was the same every morning: I was turned before the day staff came to give the red, gray-centered bony points on my body time to resume their normal coloring, thus offering clear evidence that the night nurse had been active, conscientious in the pursuit of his duty, and had not been sleeping instead of keeping watch over the thirty or so men who snored, cursed, howled or simply, like myself, lay awake under his care. I heard the click of his cigarette lighter somewhere up the dormitory and, save for the sound of his sharp inspirations, all was now quiet in this the quietest hour of the night. The heavy, hot, young man smoked on in ignorance of the fact that he had missed the man in the bed next to mine.

I should not normally have concerned myself with this man, a new admission, come during the night, weepy and passive as he emptied his pockets and stripped off the clothes which the night nurse dropped in a black plastic bag and carted off somewhere, I don't know where. I believe I had been asleep, really sleeping, for a few minutes, maybe an hour or two, rare for me, when I woke to see the new man, a ghostly gray in the whispery blue of the night light, gray the same as everything in that light, blade between thumb and forefinger, pummeling at his cheek and neck with a quiet, enduring commitment, lining his stubbled skin, letting out occasional soft gasps before he weakened and laid himself to sleep, to die, the light catching as black the blood which ran down him and disappeared under the sheet.

I, of course, would be to blame for this man's demise. Somehow I would be at fault, as surely as if I had stolen from my bed and murdered the fellow myself. Me. The stiff one, old clay-boots with his clay head and his old clay balls, a scarcely breathing hotchpotch of hair, skin and bone, who flexed not the smallest extremity, not even a toe, who lay all night like a corpse himself, who had not spoken a word in anyone's living memory—me, I would be to blame for the nurse's failure to rest a finger on that short blade the man had somehow secreted into the locker between his bed and mine. They might even try to say I had put it there myself.

And yet somehow I would have to accept that, perhaps, in the way all things that happen in this world melt together, are responsible for their reshaping, reincarnation as other events, other causes, yes, somehow, I might have been at fault over this man's death. I had never seen him before, it is true, but I would accept whatever retribution was to come my way, for that way one survived, endured, lived on, for what it was worth.

I watched the plain gray curtains and thought about the man at my back. In the hospital grounds a peacock screeched and the blood in my veins moved an inch or two. The daylight seemed early and strong and the curtains became patterned with houses or cathedrals or something. Then they came, the day staff, at the end of the dormitory, their jocularity masking the loathing they felt at having to face another day in this place. After an agony of time one came closer, was behind me saying, "Fuck," before he ran soft-footed for his colleagues.

The Head Nurse arrived, I could smell him behind me, and before drawing the curtain that divided the man's bed from my own he snapped, "Get him out of here," this being the signal for two dark-suited young men to be upon me in an instant, chasing time the way a dog, I believe, chases its own tail. They worked in a frenzy, squeezing my crackling wrists, hauling me up from the bed, slamming empty locker drawers as they took it in turns to glean for clothing. Soon they were pushing my poker arms into a shirt and a pullover, the rightful owners of which I did not know. They decided against a tie, an item of clothing easily ignored in times of haste, then one hugged me tightly from behind while the other yanked up my trousers lined, as always, with a fat incontinence pad. Socks, shoes, and I was "done."

They put me in a wheelchair, naturally, for how else, if you were so inclined, would you shift a creature such as I? They had long ago, it seemed, given up the pretense of trying to rehabilitate me, struggling daily to try and get me to bear my own weight, feed myself, wipe my own ass. No one seemed more than superficially bothered, and I was happy to have it that way. It seemed as if they had contented themselves with the fact that I still lived, somehow, in spite of my thanatophile appearance and demeanor. So I was carted around in a wheelchair, naturally. Easier. For all concerned.

■ 3 ■

In their worry for haste these two young men became unnecessarily aggressive, slamming my bad bones into the chair
when it would have been just as easy to let me drop. How
badly they wanted me out of the way, out of the dormitory to
some unused corner of the ward, or even some other part of
this rambling hospital; if it had been any later in the morning
I am sure they would have sent me straight to work in the
Industrial Unit without a thought that I had had no breakfast,
meager though my intake of food was. At times like this they
were inclined to show a certain impiety. "What shall we do
with him?" asked one. "We could put him outside," came the
reply. "Or in the toilet. Anywhere. It doesn't really matter."
The two of them broke into a relief of laughter. Boys, they
were just boys. I knew, however, that their real wish was to
be back at the dead man's side, watching, morbidly intrigued
no doubt, hopeful of catching sight of some protruding piece
of artery which they might be able to name and so impress
the Head Nurse. In their giddy indecision they left me at the
windowed entrance to the ward—hardly an indiscreet place
—before running back to the dormitory. At any other time I
found that place comforting—since I was so prominent, I was
curiously ignored by all who passed by me, each assuming,
perhaps, that I was the responsibility of someone else. From
there I could spend whole hours watching the grounds, wondering at the gardens and their outlines, the rockeries and
lawns stepped at mystifying, useless levels. I could see the
gardeners unload long-handled tools from their barrow to
begin, uncommittedly, turning the cold caked earth in the
barren flower beds. I could fretfully guess at the business of
other hospital staff, residents too, as they slouched, jaunted,
ran before me, not that their doings should have been any
concern of mine—what difference did it make to me? Still, it
was a nice game, though not one I could indulge myself with
on this particular morning. The sight before me pained my
eyes: a thick icing of snow had fallen, gently, furtively, it
seemed, to surprise all those asleep in the windless night. A
few people were about, their faces bleached and gladdened

by the snow, but they paid me no attention as they slithered past the ward, ignorant of the drama within. The dirty white and scarlet livery of an ambulance caught my eye as it bobbled at a funereal pace past the Infirmary, moving away at first then traveling laterally, past the laundry where the early steam of the day was being gobbed from vents in its long, windowless walls. The vehicle turned toward me, heading straight for me, slowly, tentatively, its front wheels probing for the limits of the road made indistinguishable from the gardens by the snow. It skidded a little as it turned to back up to the ward. Two women climbed out, opened the back and heaved a stretcher-trolley down to the ground and up to the ward doors. Someone ran from the adjacent office rattling an unneeded bunch of keys, saying, "This way. In the dormitory." The two women followed, a grainy urgency etched in their faces which I had not been able to detect through the panes of glass and the film of freezing mist that hung above the snow. The doors were left open for the cold to needle my cheeks and finger my ankles. Indifferent patients ambled down from the dormitory in search of cigarettes. One asked me if I had any, then was already on his way before he had finished his sentence. Soon, from the furthest corner of my field of vision—a reddened and greened extremity that was part reality, part supposition—I saw the party returning from the dormitory with the man hoisted over a shoulder, or suspended by the neck, or so it seemed. But this was simply an illusion, or a delusion, I could not decide which for my judgment is poor in such matters. What I saw was a huge bag of blood feeding into the body on the stretcher. Fools, I thought, letting blood to a dead man. What did he want with blood? But then, when he reached me, I heard him whimper, groan like the wind in the trees, and I realized he was still alive.

The group paused before me. Was sentence about to be passed on my part in this whole sorry affair? "What's he doing here?" growled the Head Nurse, who must have had a name, I realize, but I am at a complete loss in trying to remember what it was. "Get him out of the way," he said. One of the staff, a girl with a remarkable harelip, whose name was Tanya, or it may have been, though it is of no consequence since any name would do, hurried to my wheelchair and pulled me back a yard to repair the slight hindrance for which I was responsible. "Further, further," yapped the Head Nurse, and Tanya drew me back another yard. She was new to the place and would soon learn that by rights she should have taken me to the dining room straight away, it would have been better for her if she had, but she paused, perhaps bravely seeking to appear somehow unafraid, somehow involved in the affair. One of the young men looked at her seriously. The two ambulance women silently shrugged off any suggestion of assistance as they handed the nearly-dead one from our company and into the back of their vehicle.

Everyone watched as the red and white doors of the ambulance shrank slowly away, turning off between the dark old buildings of the hospital and out of the grounds. Then the Head Nurse broke the silence and the stillness, locking and bolting the ward doors with deliberation.

"Right," he said. "You all know what time it is. Get among them. Breakfasts. Quickly."

▪ T W O ▪

THUS THE NEW man had been taken from us leaving a hole in my mind that had not been there before. I was slipping, had known it for some time—I could not hope to live a life such as mine and expect to be completely unaffected.

It would be unfortunate if I were to dwell too long on this man whose affairs were his own and whose actions, in truth, are only incidental to this, whatever it is, my story, my confession, my last hope. I did not know him personally, though what I saw of his face seemed familiar. I could not be said to know anyone personally unless you were to count those in daily physical contact with me who pinched me to see if I winced, who dragged me here and there bidding me, "Lift your arm, do this, do that, do try Peter (that they say is my name, though I have my doubts)." No, I knew no one, least of all this newly cut, not dead man. And those that did see me, enacted their business with me, plied their trade as it were, did they ever pause to wonder at this flaky receptacle that passed for a body, to ask themselves if there was any kind of a soul inside, bearing witness to the suns and moons that passed before its eyes? Too much, I am feeling sorry for myself again and it simply will not do—I cannot afford such silly, empty sentiment. I must return to the toil of recalling the events of that day, that gaudy bauble that hangs yet aloft in the dark vault of my head, waiting, tinkling and dangling, refusing to go away until I have reached for it. Now I stretch and pull it down for you and I see it bright and terrible in my poor mind's eye. And there are more. I come across them from time to time in some forgotten abyss at the end of some innocent-looking tunnel. They are often tarnished, given to disappearing before my eyes, and sometimes I wish they had not been disturbed but left to sink in the mud rather than come to light to mock and dismay me with their cheap appearance and unreasoned array. But they go nowhere, simply hide, lie in wait, displaced but not destroyed.

On this day, then, I had thoughts only for the repercussion of the man's actions among the staff. I sensed I was to be implicated, ah God, I knew I was. Their wish to find a scapegoat for the night nurse's inefficiency would be irresistible. All day on all of the days they were ever mindful of each other, fretting over their various ranks, careful of their appearance in the eyes of the outside world, and incidents like this served only to unite them in seeking reprisal in advance of any allegations made against them. And their extraordinary conclusion in this case would be that I was to blame.

Tanya sighed heavily behind me as she pushed me into the dining room thinking, perhaps, that she too, in her newness, her conspicuous unfamiliarity with the ways of the ward, would also, somehow, have to absorb part of this unhappiness, this agitation which changed the color of the air, which was irrational and frightening. The daily routine was in a loathsome chaos—halfway through the morning and not a breakfast had been served nor a pill dispensed. In the cheerless, spotless dining room arguments were brewing between some of my fellow residents, with disjointed insults and the gobbledygook of our kind being garbled into tabletops and against cream-glossed walls. Some, having helped themselves, sat behind mountainous servings of scrambled egg, some eating, some wondering if they should dare. It would be a bad day all round and I would be glad when it was over, I seem to remember thinking. Staff appeared, drafted in from other wards, marching through the doors, their very presence placating the unrest as they seated men at tables, gently but firmly asked for quiet, then began dishing food out from the trolley. Tanya went to it and filled a bowl with the watery residue of the egg which that day would serve as my breakfast. This, as with all my food, was given to me by means of a large syringe inserted into the side of my mouth where once there had been teeth. Since my tongue was a dead thing, resting, glued to the bottom of my mouth, I had developed a contractural action using the back of my throat which worked in relation to my breathing out, allowing the passage of small amounts of fluid into my stomach. I did not ask for more, nor did I seem to need it, and this satisfied the staff too since they could be seen to be doing their best with a difficult case, sustaining him with, as they saw it, intense individual attention. My belly growled as the lukewarm, bitty fluid burned a little track down my throat.

Soon slowcoaches and malingerers feigning illness were being chivied and got ready for the trek through the snow to the Industrial Unit. I too attended this place every weekday, and Tanya wheeled me back to the locked ward doors where she left me to go in search of a coat. She returned and, with the assistance of one of the young men, began prizing the ridiculously short garment over my arms, for I was tall if not too fleshily endowed. Then we were out, a party of twelve or so, Tanya with us as one of the more compliant patients pushed me through the slush, against razored blasts of wind, under yellow clouds penciled with gray.

The industrial workshop was an airy modern annex to an old wing of the main building. It smelled of something burning faintly nearby. It was set somewhere off the square at the center of the hospital, exactly where I forget—it is of no consequence. Inside, that morning, as on every morning, patients from other wards were already at their benches, or making innumerable trips to the toilets, or drinking water from an oily sink at the end of the workshop, or scouring the floors in their insatiable pursuit of cigarette butts which they would reroll in strips of newspaper. Tanya began taking our men's coats to put them on the already groaning pegs near the door when the IU Supervisor, I forget his name, Quinn I think, appeared, grumbling. "They can manage for themselves. They know where to hang their coats. Except for that one," he said pointing a freshly-lit cigarette at me. He watched with his customary bemusement as Tanya struggled with my too-small coat. "Here," he said as he came over. "Like this." He gave a sudden violent jerk on my sleeve to free my flaccid arm. "Thank you," said Tanya blushing. "You're late," said Quinn. "It'll be docked from their pay."

I was wheeled to a table on which was a pile of white carrier bags. In a little cage on one corner of the table was a ball of string from which one man pulled and measured individual lengths between two screws in the tabletop before cutting them and laying them in the center of the table. Next to him was an old woman who threaded the string into the tops of the carrier bags, knotting it to make a handle. Two men opposite performed the same task. Another, younger woman circulated about the table and my wheelchair collecting each carrier bag as it was finished, placing them on a stool, slipping a piece of paper between each ten until she had a pile of a hundred that she would scurry away with down the workshop. "Good morning Peter," said the old woman at the table. "Aren't you going to say 'good morning' to us, then, Peter?" "He," said the man opposite, "never says anything, doesn't Peter. Got his head screwed on, knows to keep his mouth shut. Best way." "That doesn't mean," said the woman, "that we should not be polite to him. I'm sure Peter has feelings, just like the rest of us and, if he could, if he wished to, I'm sure he would be delighted to say 'good morning' to us and wish us all the very best of good wishes." "Humph," said the man.

So began my morning's "work," though of course I took no physical part in this activity. At the end of each week our productivity was measured by the number of carrier bags which had been strung, and Quinn, with some amusement, stuck a small brown envelope with coins in the bottom into my hand where it remained until I was returned to the wards where the Head Nurse took it from me for depositing in some kind of account I was meant to have. Each week, every day of each week, was just the same, though the weekends were free.

That morning, as he did every morning, one of the men stringing the carrier bags began to grumble about the wispy, obsessional woman collecting them up. "Why," he asked, "doesn't she wait until we've done a few? That way she could take them all at once and save herself work." The woman lifted the latest carrier bag from near his elbow. The man snatched it back. "Wait, damn you, why don't you wait?" She tussled silently with him, her wide eyes pleading for the carrier bag she was stretching for. Grudgingly he relented and she shuffled off to the pile with her prize. "See Peter," the old woman said to me, "see how they behave. They got no respect for each other, no manners, not like you and me."

I wondered where Tanya was. In Quinn's office, no doubt, where he would be making her giggle with weird stories, might even at that moment be passing a fingertip over her harelip, smiling at its contours, saying, "I know someone who might be able to fix that for you. At a price."

Once, one evening when they had forgotten to take me back to the ward, Quinn came up to me in the workshop, two excitable young patients at his side. He began thumbing through a magazine he had with him which was full of photographs of naked women and men. "Let's see," he said, "Let's see." When he found what he was looking for, he held the magazine open inches in front of my eyes. "Maybe this'll shift him," he said, "snap him out of whatever's supposed to be the matter with him. Come on stone-brain, look at that. How about that for a nice juicy cunt?" he said. "Bet you've never seen one like that before, eh, stone-brain? No sir, bet you've never even seen one before. What do you think boys?"

His two companions giggled nervously, obligingly. Then Quinn became more serious, tossing the magazine aside and pushing his leathery face right up to mine. "What makes you think you're so special?" he hissed. Then he smiled again, a hard, empty smile, as he reached down and pulled open the top of my trousers. "Any life down here I wonder?" he said, guffawing, reaching for my prick. "Anything stirring down there, Peter m'boy?"

But he froze before he had reached far enough, halted, certainly, by the same secret doubt I had seen in others, the querulous look and fear that asked, Is there yet someone alive in that shell? Some living human being, watching, waiting to come back to life to seek retribution against those who wronged him in his time of indisposition? Might there yet be some ember that could burst suddenly into flame, escaping, falling away to earth like a maggot dropping from a carcass?

Quinn's behavior meant nothing to me—I had long since stopped feeling threatened by such as he. I was no longer afraid, quite used to it, in fact; had been for, I don't know, a very long time, as long a time as it takes to forget fear.

One of the patients came round with the tea-trolley. On it were blue cups containing sugared tea and orange cups containing unsugared. And one syringe.

But I was not to receive this drink.

The telephone rang in Quinn's office and behind the frosted-glass partition I could just make out Tanya's turquoise-clad figure as she jumped up and came to the door. She began pulling on her coat. Quinn, belly jutting, stood in the doorway, eyeing her up and down from behind as she jinked her way through this daft circus he called his workshop. A sense of fate jabbed somewhere in my chest as I realized she was coming toward me. Then she was beside me, slight, dark, a little ugly, reaching for the brakes on the wheelchair. "We must go back to the ward," she said. "You have a visitor."

THREE

HOW MISERABLE I was becoming—not like me—on this wretched, wretched day. Sunlight lasered through the clouds and filled my eyes with yellow blindness as Tanya wheeled me through the slush back to the ward, saying nothing, contemplating, perhaps, the fact that she too would be apprehended over this new mistake. And I? Who could say what would happen to me now. More time wasted, and my work time to boot. Ah, that I could feign illness, send a luminescent green flush from my nose, sweat at will, change the color of my skin. My ancient wish of becoming invisible stirred itself again—though I never really wanted to be completely invisible. It was just my head which, from time to time, I longed to have removed from my shoulders and placed on the end of a string, to have it dangled in my pocket that I might still hear, yet not bear full witness to, the musterings around me.

I never had visitors. My family, if any were still alive, had certainly forgotten or disowned me a very long time ago. Maybe this was all just a joke, played for Tanya's benefit or designed as the punishment itself for my own alleged part in the events of the previous night. I had known such behavior, but this did not seem to me a day for lightheartedness.

She wheeled me straight into the ward office, a room I could not remember entering since my transfer to that ward some long time before. How often I had longed to be in that hot nerve-center with its row of filing cabinets standing like tombstones and its drug trolley chained to the wall. Somewhere in that room was my history. Was it slim? Was it a big fat folder crammed with explanation about the way I was, the chances of my becoming any different, be it for better or worse? I fancied the pages, if there were any, would all be blank, yellowing at the edges; that would seem fitting, somehow. My many medicine cards would be there since I had, up until quite recently, been the recipient of a great range of tranquilizers, antidepressants, and vitamin pills which had to be crushed; and there would have to be the record of my electrical treatment, tried and dropped many times over the years. But I still fantasized about the eradication of even these basic entries in favor of white empty pages that told all they really knew about me. Yet I cannot deny that I craved to hear their exchanges about me in this their jealously guarded, private cell. Here the handovers took place between the shifts, twice a day, when all the patients were discussed. Could there possibly be great elaborate plans for me, culled from details prepared from their secret observations? I had often wondered about a small red light in the dormitory ceiling, and the clock on the dayroom wall: were not its thirty-second clicks remarkably similar to the sound made by a camera shutter? Could there be wires in the walls? I had contemplated often, with distressing inconclusiveness, that there might be no other earthly reason for their taking me to the toilet, as they did now and again, and leaving me there for hours, except for the purpose of spying on me in isolation. I know, I know, these are not the thoughts of a rational man. Indeed, if I had heard these theories expressed by anyone I should immediately have categorized them as brilliantly typical of a certain kind of person with whom I shared residence. But I had much time on my hands, and too little by way of diversion. Though salvation was sometimes close by, usually when I least expected it, for I had often been left near the office by a hurrying nurse and, now and again, I had overheard some of the most comforting words of my whole life filtering through the half-open door at handover time: "Peter? Nothing new. What do you expect? No change, no change at all." And since I believe mine was always the last name on the list I took even greater reassurance from seeing the receiving shift already leaving the office when I was up for discussion. But nothing lasts, no such thing as eternity; time came and eroded my frail sense of security, leaving me to mull my predicament all over again. Indeed, that very morning, that very minute as I thought about the existence of my history, I became unduly puzzled over the recent withdrawal of my medication, to which I had not previously given a moment's thought.

A tiring heat poured from two radiators either side of me. I felt a sudden nostalgia for the Industrial Unit, even for Quinn, as the Head Nurse took over from Tanya, twisting and reversing the wheelchair in swift, jerky movements so that it stood at right angles to the desk which dominated the office. The heat was monstrous after the cold outside, and I feared I would be sick. It was no good messing someone like me about this way. I would have to swallow my vomit, perhaps choke to death on it there and then, for it would never come out.

Behind the desk sat an elderly, palsied-faced man, a methodically dressed man whom I did not recognize at first in my lathery confusion, but soon realized was Beckerminster, a doctor, my doctor, my consultant, judge and jury, a maker of decisions. So it was before him I was now being brought to account for my aberrations and misdoings. And my guilt descended on me like night—I was to blame for whatever crime they chose to charge me with; and it was with my customary silence that I would have to accept the verdict and sentence passed by this distinguished man who glanced at me briefly, sniffed, then set his eyes back to the desk on which was a webby folder. My history? Read to me. Let me see. No. I did not really want to know what was scrawled on those pages in many different hands, in untidy paragraphs dated back to God knows when.

The Head Nurse stood at Beckerminster's side. The only sound in the room was the rustling of the pages of my history. Then Beckerminster gargled and spoke. "Are you sure you have the, er, authority? Shouldn't I have some say in the matter? After all, I am the fellow's doctor, the responsible medical officer, so to speak. And, you know, the prognosis is damnably poor. Wouldn't you prefer more pliable material? Someone more amenable to the kind of service you offer? He seems happy enough here. Quite stable. Been the same for years. I have to be careful. Ethics and all that. It would not do to make the wrong decision. The man does not speak for himself, therefore we must act on his behalf and hope we are fulfilling his best interests. I've heard a little about your work. Rumor mostly. Much of it may be quite untrue, but I am led to believe that your methods are very avant-garde. Correct me if I am being injudicious, but isn't your approach to mental instability rather experimental and unverified as yet? I cannot permit my patients to be used as guinea pigs, you must appreciate that."

He looked away over my shoulder to a point from where a woman's creamy voice descended as if from the ether, saying, "Dr. Beckerminster, forgive me, but it hardly seems 'ethical' to be discussing someone's life, his history and destiny, right under his nose, while behaving as if he were not even in the same building. Isn't that right Peter?" She placed her hands on my shoulders and leaned forward to show me a stiff smile. She was dark-haired, middle-aged, no, twenty-something, I've really no idea. "I am afraid," she said, "that it is part of our operational and budgetary directive to take a case such as Peter's." She stood in front of me, cupping a hand over my temple and squinting into my eyes. "You don't mind if I just have a good look at you, do you, Peter?" She stood behind me again and lifted my arms above my head, lowered them and lifted them until my joints began to burn. From a bag on the desk she took a pair of dividers and rolled up my trouser leg to pinch and measure the thin ribbon that passed for a calf muscle. She prodded my carotid, then stood back, looking thoughtfully at me. "What kind of creature are you, Peter?" she asked. "How do we describe your state, your malady?

Are you psychotic? Traumatized? Hysterical? A sad case? Or are you simply having us all on? Tell me, Peter, are you, perhaps, nothing more than an old fraud?"

"Really!" said Beckerminster. "There's no need for that. The man has feelings . . ." "Does he?" the woman retorted. "We had a similar case only last year. Our techniques proved a resounding success. The details were well chronicled. The Kaufmann case. Have you heard of it, doctor?" "Yes," said Beckerminster, "and I also heard of the man's subsequent suicide." "Mmmm," said the woman. "Unfortunately the after-care service did not match the acute stages of the treatment." Beckerminster, this good, owlish man, looked dismayed, the smeared features of his face lined like stone. The woman turned to the Head Nurse asking, "When did he last bear his own weight?" Then, before waiting for an answer, she leaned into me, sliding her hands under my armpits and, with an unexpected strength, she hauled me from my seat, hugging me to her, my head lolling down on her shoulder as she wriggled her arms about my waist, bouncing me up and down on my flailing feet before tiring and dropping me heavily, back into the chair. Her forehead was moist, like my own, and she inhaled quietly, deeply, unsuccessfully attempting to hide her momentary fatigue. "I am not happy," said Beckerminster. "Not happy at all." "I can insist," said the woman. "You know that. Surely," she said, "surely you could use the bed? Is the world not littered with mildly depressed unfortunates, all sobbing into their pill bottles, pleading for sanctuary in a nice place like this? Such patients can be 'cured,' you know that. And what happy statistics they make when they are sent home, never to darken your door again. And think, are you not being somewhat negligent in your service of the best interests of this patient by refusing him the only method of treatment available for such as he? What more can you possibly do for him here?"

She paced the floor, dominating the room with her tallness and her elegance.

"Perhaps," she said, "in view of your reluctance to discharge this man into our care, we could come to some other arrangement. How about leave? Six weeks or so? I could demand more if I wanted. Wouldn't that suit you, Head Nurse? An empty bed for a while? Less work for your famously beleaguered staff?"

The Head Nurse, his lower lip protruding, avoided her look and made no reply.

"All right, all right," Beckerminster said with soft metal in his voice. "Have him. Trial period. We'll say a month, shall we?"

The woman smiled, looked at me, and nodded.

The Head Nurse tapped on the window of the office door and beckoned the two boys who had dressed me that morning.

"Bath for this one," he said, gesturing to me. "Now," he said, "and look lively. Then get his property together. He's going out."

The two boys looked at him, their expressions absorbing some small, certain disbelief I too detected in the tone of his voice.

"Well?" he said, his throat squeaking. "What are you waiting for?"

"Nothing," they replied, seizing the chair and making off with me down the corridor.

F O U R

SOMETIMES I THINK I must be going mad. I had got
it wrong, completely wrong. Certainly my presence beside
the attempted suicide had irritated them that morning, and it
is true that if they could have remedied the situation by taking their anger out on me in some way, they would have
done just that. But I was not to blame, not really, and by the
time they had bathed me, combed my hair, filched clothes for
me from other patients' lockers and sat me in the wheelchair
with a box of incontinence pads in my lap, I could see that
they genuinely did not want me to go in the company of this
woman who clicked primly along the ward corridor, my history in a big brown envelope under her arm. Why, even the
Head Nurse himself came to the woman's small white car to
help lift me into the passenger seat, standing by, picking hairs
from his gray suit while one of the boys pulled the seat belt
tight across my ribs and middle. I had underestimated him
and Beckerminster, and became filled with a vague, cloying
emotion. My removal from the hospital was a totally separate
incident, wholly unconnected with the business concerning
the man in the next bed. I had it all wrong and once more
was given to worrying about my sanity.

The woman climbed in beside me, tossing her bag, and my
history, onto the back seat. Without a sign to the attendant
party she started the car and we traveled away, out of the
hospital grounds, distance suddenly appearing between us
and the only home I had known in God knows how many
years. The sun was low and dazzling. Hot air came up from

somewhere near my feet—they would burn after a while, I thought. I felt a momentary attack of the nausea I had experienced in the ward office, but it soon dissipated and disappeared. We passed through a town where I saw bright awnings above shop windows, bottles of milk on the doorsteps of damp-bricked houses, children, lorries and cars that made me feel giddy and prevented my eyes from blinking. As we made our way out into the country the woman leaned forward over the wheel, smiling. Her name, she said, was Anna.

Her voice seemed softer than it had in the office. "You," she said, "may not be used to people addressing you directly. It's not your fault. Just put it down to the inadequacies of the institution. Then forget all about the place. Forget how you were manhandled without a word, talked about as if you were some dumb animal. I know your type, Peter, and I know you're in there somewhere, listening to me, wondering, naturally, what you have been let in for. Where you are going you will be treated with respect, and we expect that you will respond accordingly. Your case is not unique, though you may have been led to believe that it is. At One World you will not be a 'case,' no, you will be, first and absolutely foremost, a human being, a living, feeling, thinking man capable of all the sweetness and essence that is given to mankind. You will act for yourself, be able to shrug off the nightmare of your past. You need only have the simplest of faith in us and you will be rewarded. We can make you well again, but you must be prepared to make the greatest effort yourself. Work, Peter, work hard, and you will be whole once more."

It was all too much for me. I fell asleep.

Across a wall, over a fast river children were juggling with black and white cones. My mouth was open and I was sure I had called to them, but they seemed to take no notice, carrying on with their game, silently and intently performing its mysterious moves. Somewhere in the wall was a glass door with a big silver lock. From some part of my body I conjured a key, but its metal was weak and it bent as I tried it in the lock. Then the keyhole was so large I found I could get what I took to be my fingers inside to flick over the tumblers. With a will I forced open the door to find the scene changed: where there had been a river and children playing I saw only a black ditch skirting a grassy expanse. I had the sensation of running over great areas of hillside but, in my dreaming eye, I saw only the image of my head, chest, shoulders and arms, floating, going nowhere. I contrived that the children should somehow reappear, but the figures which ghosted up before me were not children; indeed, I had become the child in their midst. They were resting, dark shapes, fatigued as if by the rigors of battle. All about them were severed limbs and other pieces of human matter. In a piece of madness I believed this offal to be the parts needed for an adult version of the game I had seen the children playing. I tried juggling the meat, but the various bits and pieces would not behave in my hands, sticking to my fingers, soiling my own apparently healthy skin. I wanted to go back, but there was nowhere to go back to. The earth fell from beneath me and I woke with a powerful headache.

We were turning from a main road on to a black side road which snaked its way before us through white fields. Anna leaned forward again to look at me, but this time she did not smile. I got the impression that she had gone on talking to me for some time before she realized I was asleep. She seemed uncomfortable; perhaps we had been traveling too long, I had no idea. The sun was no longer so apparent, being shaded by ivory clouds which diffused its light and made its whereabouts vague. Anna remained silent as she turned the car into an area of woodland. Then I was struck by an amusing thought: Was all this simply an elaborate charade? Were we to meet accomplices of hers who would drag me from the car, cover me with leaves and soil that I might be claimed by the earth, weathered and eaten by insects, acids, moonlight? Was I about to die? No one on this planet would know, certainly no one could be that bothered. If there had been muscles in my face I might have smiled at that thought. I wondered if I really cared myself.

"Nearly there," she said from somewhere remote, way outside my field of concentration, her words turning and waking something in my mind. On the right of the rough gravel track which we were traveling along a white house appeared, truly white, though its roof was covered with snow and seemed to be made of some kind of thatch. A sign informing no conceivable traffic stated, in gold on black, "One World Intensive Rehabilitation Center." Snow had formed crescents in the upstairs windows making the house look like a many-eyed startled face glaring beyond us at some distant, unseeable horror as we passed up the short drive to the front door. A man stepped out, a tubby, short man, bespectacled, untidy brown hair swept back from his forehead. He nodded at Anna. "Excuse me, Peter," she said forcedly. "I shall just be a few minutes. You had better wait here."

By now they would be happy, the staff back at the hospital, flying in their happiness over their momentary, genuine regret at my being taken out of their care. And to add to their happiness no guilt could be attached to them. since it had not been their decision that I should go. They would be free, feeling free of me, the stiffy, the one who stuck out amongst the moving ones, those amenable to the treatment they offered, those who could at least hold some kind of a conversation or take themselves off to the toilet. I, the clayboots, the old rock that littered the ward, was no longer among them, frustrating them in their work; and now they would appear an iota more modern, my place available for a more hopeful case. But it would not have done for me to have been angry with them. I could not afford anger, it might have made me do something I would regret, if that were at all possible. I had my moments though, I admit, late at night perhaps, when I would lie in my wet bed, screaming in my skull for the darkness to come and make a mess of me, have done with me, turn me to water, to powder, to spirit me away into nothing, finish me for good. Then this fiery sentiment would die and I would be left, days later perhaps, clinging to life in the same pathetic way I had craved my own demise.

Anna exchanged words with the man, he nodding expressionlessly, she occasionally opening her hands as if going through some process of self-justification. The two fell silent and he looked at me, staring through the glass of the windscreen at me, absorbed in his quiet thoughts; then he disappeared back inside the house. Anna shuddered, hugged herself, and her breath was a white flame on the cold air.

FIVE

PRESENTLY AN OLD man in a grubby cream apron appeared, trundling a wheelchair from the back of the house. Anna moved smartly to the side of the car and opened the door. "Right Tom," she said, "if you take him at the top and I grab his legs, OK?" Their hands reached into the car, tangling with each other, fumbling with the seat belt, feeling for their quarry. "Come on, Peter," said the old man, his nose moist and capillaried. "Into this chair," he said. "But don't get too used to it, mind." He grinned, his lips thin and pink, as he took my weight, hoisting me into the wheelchair before bending back into the car for the black polythene bag containing my "belongings." He put the bag in my lap and curled my hand over it. Then he reached back into the car for my history which he handed to Anna. The bag slid from under my moist palm, creased shirts and odd socks spilling onto the slushy gravel. A shadow of irritation passed over his face before he bent down to pick up my things. "Never mind, Peter," he said. "Never you mind."

As they wheeled me round to the back of the house I felt a curious sensation: the building had jerked, slipped somehow, bounced a little in its foundations. But the other two seemed to have noticed nothing and I readily attributed it to my considerable fatigue. Tom negotiated a troublesome step with the chair, pushing me into a big, warm kitchen dominated by two yellow-topped tables pushed together in the center. The place was alive with the smell of freshly baked food and my stomach stirred unpleasantly. "Has he eaten?"

asked Tom. Anna silently and tartly indicated that he should direct his question to me. "I'm sorry," he said to her, compounding his error. "Have you had anything to eat Peter?" he bawled, unnecessarily. The two looked down at me in silence. Anna pursed her lips. "They've been using a syringe to feed him," she said. "Too long-term for a nasogastric tube, we must presume. We shall have to adopt their method for the moment. Can you fix something up? A funnel and a piece of tubing, perhaps?" "I should be able to manage," said Tom. Anna left, clutching her bag and my history.

The old man went quietly about his business, pausing to smile at me occasionally, opening and closing cupboard doors, holding various tins of food inches from my eyes. "You'll soon get used to us here," he said. "Us and our little ways. Have you back on your feet in no time. I'm guessing that you like baked beans. Never met anyone who doesn't. Soon find out what you like and what you don't, eh?" he said as he opened the tin. "All your likes, ah, and all your little dislikes."

He never tired of this vacuous chatter all through the preparation of the meal he mashed and watered and poured into a clear plastic bottle from which he fed a piece of red tubing. He poked a finger into my mouth, cleverly finding the side where there were no teeth. Then he inserted the tube and began squeezing, very gently at first, I noticed, as the salty mixture dripped into my mouth and burnt my tongue. Then he became too ambitious and squeezed the inverted bottle harder, too hard for my complex swallowing mechanism to cope with. I gagged and spewed the mixture back through my nose. He stood back looking briefly disappointed and at the same time concerned as he glanced at the door through which Anna had left then back to me. After a few awkward seconds in which he seemed at a loss as to what he should do, he looked down at my chest and put his nose in front of my mouth to satisfy himself I was not asphyxiating. He mopped the sick from my face and clothes with a towel he left to soak in a bucket of hot water. "So," he said, "you're not keen on old Tom's cooking? Never mind. Not to worry, not to worry at all. We'll soon sort something out, won't we? Tell you what, let's go and find your room. They should have decided where you'll be sleeping by now. I'll bet you're dying to see it. Yes?"

He pushed me into a dark, carpeted hall, the floorboards creaking under the wheels of the chair, past a staircase to a room I guessed served as some kind of reception or office. From inside the room came a garbled discussion between Anna and, I assumed, the man who had come out to meet her on our arrival. Tom stood at my side, listening, dropping all pretense of paying me direct attention. He leaned toward the door, cocking his head, thin daylight lightening the dark hollows beneath his eyes. Was this old man worried that the two inside were talking about him? A chair scraped the floor in the room, footsteps came near and Tom snapped out of his trance and knocked.

The old man, an ex-patient somehow employed by the Center, need not have worried. He wheeled me into the office. My history lay open on a desk. The atmosphere was hot, dense, and I could almost taste the antagonism between Anna and the man who stared out of the window, his back to us, refusing to acknowledge our entrance. "My name," he said, addressing the snow on the drive beneath the window, "is John. I am the Director of the One World Rehabilitation Center." He snorted, turned and came over to me. He leant forward, lifting his glasses to take a closer look, then stepped back a pace perturbed, no doubt, by the redolence of vomit on my clothes and faint breath. He seemed to cool a little at this, as if obscurely impressed. He then went through a seemingly practiced speech explaining the function of the "house," its policy of taking unusual and difficult cases which ordinary mental hospitals had neither the time, will, nor specialist techniques to tackle effectively. He went on to explain that they were about to formulate a contract to which I would be obliged to adhere and which gave a structure to my "treatment," such, he said, as it might be. He was trying his hardest to be professional, even convivial, but I had the strong impression that I was not the kind of material he wanted in "his house." Anna was to blame. She had chosen badly and his record would suffer, though he would not be able to return me to the hospital without some token effort: that would have made a dreadful smear on his record, his accountability to, well, whoever.

Tom, as if the recipient of some reprieve, was cheerful, lighthearted as we left the office. He dragged the chair up the two half-flights of stairs and along a dark, creaking landing to the room which I had been allotted. Inside was a single bed, carpet and curtains, a washbasin, a wardrobe and two chests of drawers, into each drawer of which he deposited single items of my luggage. The wind rapped on the roof of the house. When he had finished he said he was leaving me for a while to let me get accustomed to my new surroundings. Anyway, he had to make tea for everyone.

I began to wonder at the space which seemed to be suddenly and irretrievably unfolding around me, pouring out of me into a void, my faint horizons broken by this day nagging at me, threatening to suck me out of myself, innards drawn through a circle of my own flesh till I was gone. Harrowing, sinister moments, real, too real to bear thinking about.

The daylight failed quickly and soon I was in complete darkness save for a narrow strip of light at the foot of the door. I listened to the strange footsteps on the landing and running along the hall downstairs. Lights were switched on and off, a television was booming somewhere, voices called, and I was remembered.

Tom appeared, or rather his hand did, snaking through the gap in the door, feeling for the light which he clicked on, only for the bulb to ping above my head putting everything back into darkness. He shuffled off and brought a replacement. "Bloody things," he said. "Don't last two minutes." He brought a chair from outside the room and stood on it to replace the bulb. He gasped as if wearied by the effort of stretching, set the chair aside, then stood and smiled at me.

"Well, Peter my boy," he said. "Getting used to us now are you? Us and our funny little ways? You'll like it here, certain of it," he said as he drew the curtains behind me.

"Now," he went on, "I'm meant to take you downstairs to meet the rest of the residents." He looked at his watch and shook his head. "I don't know, though; it is getting rather late and I think you've probably had enough excitement for one day. What do you say? Yes? No? Am I right? Plenty of time for all that tomorrow. Yes? We don't want to rush things, now, do we? Shouldn't expect too much of you on your first day, though I can tell you've made quite an impression already, yes my boy, quite an impression indeed. Anyway, time you were thinking about sleep, you've another day ahead of you tomorrow."

From outside the room he brought a newly procured syringe filled with warm milk which he allowed to trickle, too slowly this time, down my throat. I spluttered and he laid the syringe aside. Then he tried to get a toothbrush between my clenched teeth, but this too was unsuccessful and in a moment of pique he threw the brush across the room into the sink. He sighed and looked to the ceiling then, without comment, began undressing me, heaving at my shirt, dragging my trousers down to reveal a stain of thick urine on the pad and my leg, the only output I could recall since leaving the hospital that morning, that eternity ago.

When I was naked and he had wiped away my mess, he heaved me onto the bed and covered me with a cold sheet and heavy blankets. He turned out the light and closed the door.

It was early in the evening, I guessed, but he had been right in suggesting that the exertions of this day might have taken their toll on me. I lay in the darkness, tense and perplexed. He had left my shoulder exposed to the cold and tomorrow it would cause me pain.

There you have it, then, this day I have described, confessed out of sight, the bauble broken, though it will always remain, hidden, its cusps and its brilliance embedded somewhere, above, below, in my liver maybe, nicking and scorching some secret part of me till I bleed, and am once more obliged to recognize its presence in my memory. And would that this was the only day I might seek to forget.

S I X

I WAS CRACKING up. Certain of it. Why couldn't they just leave me alone? Renegades. Cunts. I was not coming apart in the mental sense, that much I felt reasonably sure about. No, this was different. You see, bits of me were breaking loose, shaking free inside, kidneys, heart, spleen, even my intestines, were all freeing themselves from their moorings, lifting their roots from the brittle shell of my body which seemed to want nothing to do with keeping its respective components in place. That business of removing me from the hospital had taken its toll. They should have known better than to fool around with someone like me. What right had they? But then, what were my rights?

I had a recurrent dream which began to impose itself on my conscious thoughts, an image of John bending over me as I lay on a mortuary slab. He lifted his glasses, straining to recognize me, knowing he should be able to put a name to this thin corpse, but he shook his head and walked away. I, in my turn, was viewing the scene from a corner of the cold room, maybe I was an attendant or something, and I too came and looked at the body, shook my head and walked away.

The day after my arrival at One World John came in search of me, full of warmth and pleasantries, perhaps in atonement for his gruff manner of the previous day. "Come," he said. "We will go outside. We have much to discuss."

A thaw had set in during the night and much of the drive and rear courtyard were wet and clear of snow. He wheeled me out beyond some outbuildings from which came the sound of men tending light machines. I heard the squirt of a motorbike passing along some distant road beyond the woods surrounding us. He stopped in a small garden, an enclosed area of small tufted lawns, a greenhouse, bare flower beds still speckled with white where the sun had not yet reached, and a pond. He took a stick and prodded at the ice floating on the top of the water. "Did you ever keep fish, Peter?" he asked. "No? I should make more time. A man in my line of work can only profit from the enhanced relaxation afforded by such a simple pastime." He smiled, his teeth nicotined and uneven. "I put four carp in here. They didn't last a week. I wonder often about the quality of the water. I have a weakness for handsome fish, but I fear the science of keeping them in perfect health baffles me."

I wished he would get to the point. He threw the stick to the opposite side of the pond then knelt down in front of me. He took my hand and warmed it between his.

"Peter, I must be frank with you. Yours is not the kind of case we should be dealing with at One World. We had one similar, a man who made a remarkable recovery, but he was not as advanced as you are. Now they seem to think we can just take all their hopeless causes and perform miracles with them. It's not like that. God, that it were so easy. Ah, dear God, that it were."

He took a handkerchief from his pocket and wiped a dew-drop from the end of his nose.

"Let me put it another way," he said. "Our techniques are under observation and there is much pressure on us to succeed. By that I mean we must be seen to cure. We have our critics, and there are those who praise us. But, as ever, it is the damning voices which ring out loudest. Do you follow me? Peter, can you understand what I'm saying? What I'm saying is that you may well hold a vital key to our future. They are watching you, bound to be, and they will want to see you progress. For us, my boy, you might try a little. Do as we ask, search your inner resources, look beyond your limits, and do something to help yourself. Do you trust me? Do you?"

He nodded to himself, stood and muttered, "Yes, I think you do," then wheeled me back to the house.

In the days that followed I gleaned more of my surroundings and particularly my fellow residents who numbered about twelve or so, though a precise count was difficult since two girls I took to be twins were in fact triplets—that is there were three not two, and their divided and coupled appearances made counting intolerably difficult. Since the house never seemed to meet as a whole I was never sure whether or not I had counted them once before. They were strikingly similar, spending much of their time flitting noisily about the house in pursuit of each other's company, changing their clothes many times in the course of a day, often wearing each other's garments. I abandoned the idea of counting. Another woman, a compulsive drinker of water, would swallow so much that she vomited, projectile fashion, often the length of a room, after which she would dutifully fetch a bucket and mop to clean up the mess, quietly and without fuss. A man sat in a corner of one lounge pulling tufts from his hair, examining them in his palm before rolling them into soft balls which he pushed into a small cloth bag he carried everywhere with him. There was another man, the Major, a tall, slim, handsome type who seemed out of place among the others. And the rest were ordinary psychiatric sorts, crazy by degrees, that I had already met before; that is, I knew their ailments better than my own, their various madnesses occupying other shells in other places of refuge I had haplessly frequented. Mostly I saw them at mealtimes since they seemed to disappear for great parts of the day to places in the house or outside where I understood some of them did some kind of work.

We all ate in the kitchen where Anna, sitting behind me, watching Tom going about the laborious business of trying to feed me, decided that I should be taken from the wheelchair and sit at the table like all the others. This Tom did by pushing me right up to the table so that I should not fall sideways or slump forward on my face. This rule was also to apply when I was taken to the lounge where, if I was lucky, I was placed in a most agreeable soft armchair.

On that first morning I was weighed then stretched out on the floor to be measured. Tom did this and all the rest of the donkey work involved in my induction into One World. He took to carrying a rolled-up copy of my "contract" in his cardigan pocket. Sometimes he would read to me from it: "In the morning you will consider your program. It is not our business to make you dependent on us. You will concentrate your every effort on helping yourself. When you wake think about your clothing. What kind of clothes will be suitable for that particular day? What would you like to wear? Would any particular item of your wardrobe appear in keeping with your current mood, or the way you view your unique personality? Think about reaching for your clothing and putting it on, even if you are yet in the stage where you might need some assistance. What other tasks will you have to perform to make yourself presentable to the day? How will you achieve those tasks?" And so on.

Mostly Tom kept it for his own reference.

In the mornings he would come into my room and sit quietly since he was meant to allow me to wake naturally. He would make some kind of notes, though whether they concerned me I never knew. However he soon grew tired of this since he had other work to do, and he also realized that though I was fully awake and might have been for the whole night, my eyes had slipped shut and would not open until he either lifted the lids himself or sat me upright on the bed. Usually he settled for the latter, pulling me up and looking quickly with a charmingly disguised distaste to see what mess I had made during the night. I was not supposed to have a drawsheet in the bed but Tom, since he was the one who had to change and wash the bedclothing, took to surreptitiously slipping a slit plastic bag between the bottom sheet and the mattress. I guess he minimalized his reports about my incontinence, which was greater than it had been at the hospital. He would prepare sheets of wet tissue in the handbasin, bringing them over, slipping a few, if he remembered, into my hand, before wiping me down and shaving my stubble. All the time he would chatter, doing his best, I admit, to try and get me to do something for myself. One morning he playfully covered me in talcum powder and I sneezed. Mildly astonished, he dived into a drawer to produce a vest which he dangled in front of me saying, "Come on Peter. Try this. See if you can put it on."

Each day he gave me an injection or two of a sickly-smelling substance which came in two brown phials and which he mixed in the syringe he rolled between his palms. He seemed to enjoy this and the homely kind of skill it took to flick the bubbles from the tops of the phials and place the needle on the syringe.

I was usually the last into the kitchen, the rest having gone about their vague business save for the odd straggler, the obsessive drinker perhaps—Tom would snatch her glass of water and send her packing. After breakfast I was taken to a small gymnasium. Tom would lay rubber mats on the floor and begin a fanciful routine whereby he picked me up, hugging me from behind, rested my heels on his feet, then began walking me. In one corner was a long mirror where I would catch our comical reflection as we turned on each circuit of the room. Since I was taller, he had to bury his head in the small of my back to keep me upright as he groaned, struggling for air, rhythmically counting to four with each effort, aimed, I would guess, at simulating the technique of walking. Sometimes Anna would come and watch, pacing the floor in her long boots, peering at us from odd angles, looking for knee flexions or any sign of voluntary movement by me, the thin scarecrow in the arms of a short, breathless old man.

In the afternoons Tom gave me hot baths and sometimes immersed my arms and ankles in a trough of melted wax before going through a series of passive movements with me, occasionally prompted by John or Anna who would come into the steamy bathroom to look at me, earnestly absorbed by the activity, pinching my skin, probing for any sign of new muscle or fat, often interrupting Tom to suggest new angles through which he might rotate my head or arms. This over, I was dressed and taken down for the evening meal, usually long before the arrival of the others to allow Tom time to start cooking and setting places.

This was a pleasant hour, the best of the day, spoilt only by the others coming in dribs and drabs, demanding, arguing, shoveling food down, and leaving to bang up the stairs, slamming doors, turning on radios. I tended to receive my meal of strong meaty extracts and syrupy sweet fluids only when time permitted between the serving and satisfying of the others. Later I would be taken to the lounge to watch television, often alone.

One evening one of the triplets wandered in, flicked through all the channels, sat for a few minutes, turned the volume up, then disappeared upstairs to change her clothes. Then the Major came in and asked, "Mind if I change the TV over, old chap?" Tall, graceful, thin-limbed, he bent over the set, turned the sound down a little and switched over.

Tom and Jerry.

Tom was bouncing Jerry back and forth on a table tennis bat to which he had him attached by a piece of elastic. Smack. Smack. Smack. The Major settled into a chair and grinned. Jerry freed himself and dashed across the room picking up an umbrella which he pitched into Tom's open mouth. The umbrella opened inside Tom's head making his face huge, spread like a parachute. Then Tom, sitting on a drop-leaf table, was propelled from the kitchen by a giant catapult. The table became transformed into an airplane, the leaves opening up for wings, and he flew round the pink living room, glaring down with narrowed eyes and pointed teeth on the fearful, running Jerry whom he bombed with a marrow released from the underside of the table. The mouse swallowed the thing whole. Gloop. He was bloated into the shape of the marrow. Tom flew out of the window and circled the house, reentering by smashing another window. The Major chuckled heavily saying, "Go on, Tom!" Jerry goaded the cat into crashing into a kitchen dresser. Tom emerged from the pile of broken crockery waving a white flag, stars spinning around his head. The Major smiled in quiet satisfaction.

· S E V E N ·

ALL RIGHT, SO what was my problem, then? Why should I get myself into such a state, make such a fuss just because people were trying to help me? What made me the way I was in the first place? Illness? Paralysis? Trauma? Maybe the last, yes, maybe, but my intransigence was not the result of an accident, not that. It was not in my mind at that time to ask myself such questions, though in the end I would be forced to look at my past, the whole dim province that lay beneath the dust and grime on the ramps and galleries of my memory.

Mostly I had begun to think about the motives of those about me who seemed so earnest in their efforts to galvanize me, metamorphose me into something fulsome, a whole appropriation of the kind of creature they believed I should be, an approximation perhaps, of themselves or the people they thought themselves to be. They, like all before them, made their decisions certain in the knowledge that they were acting in my best interests. And it came easily to them, for I did not, could not, speak up in my own defense.

I had, it seemed, come to take my stillness and the comfort I found there, too much for granted. Yes, that was it—I had become complacent, too happy with my lot, and now I was being made to account for it. I had no inalienable right to contentment, I knew that, but these people were taking great exception to me and it looked as if they were not going to rest until they had come up with some permanent arrest of my catatonic state.

I put on weight. Not much, just a few pounds I think, but even that was contrary to the general wasting process to which I had become peacefully resigned. And I had sneezed of course, but that was neither here nor there. Sometimes I felt ill, nauseous, but I guessed there was something in the injections I received to suppress my ability to vomit, a tactic opted for, no doubt, on the very first day of my arrival when I had so ungraciously rejected Tom's first efforts at feeding me. The house with its many small rooms, heavy wide doors, angled windows, mirrors and paintings, seemed to be absorbing me in some way, pressing in on me, constricting, trying to digest me, always watchful. At night I would lie awake and listen to the winter wind scratching around in the woodland outside, lifting the dead leaves, making the trees crackle like fire, and I would wonder if I should ever leave the place alive. In my dreams I began to see them reaching for me, probing inside my skull with their clever fingers, teasing at my innards, producing a wayward organ by some trick, some sleight of hand which did not require incision of my flesh. And they would talk to me and baffle me with indecipherable conundrums.

I began to long for the hospital, its patchy discipline, its superficial concern for its own survival, its watery formality and poor standards, its inability to justify itself in the things that it did and the way that it did them. I could hide there, whether I was alone or in the company of thirty other men. I was invisible, dare I say inviolate, and they could not reach me, did not want to, save for the odd token gesture for appearance's sake. But it was different at One World. John and Anna were ambitious, apparently insatiable in their pursuit of "improvement" in my "condition." There was no mention of my being sent back to the hospital. Where would it all end? More importantly, how could I escape? I could not, of course; I could only endure. I would eat, I would shit, feel the cold, but after all there was no other option for me but to endure.

I had one course of action open to me: I could refuse the

food. By letting my tongue thicken I could fill my mouth and Tom could not get the nozzle of the tubing he used properly inserted. The method was effective. At breakfast, one morning, bits of liquidized cereal oozed from my lips, not a drop swallowed. Likewise with the lukewarm sweet tea. Tom accepted it all quietly. I had wonderful visions of my skeletal frame being strapped to a stretcher and carted back to the hospital. At lunchtime, when everyone else had eaten and gone, I prepared myself for a repeat of this routine. Anna came into the kitchen. She was carrying an overtly displayed clear plastic bag full of purple sachets. Tom had his back to me. He was warming soup on the stove. Anna ordered him to start his feeding ritual. I felt very happy, now having a senior and influential audience to impress. Tom gently squeezed the meaty mixture into my mouth and it duly reappeared between my lips, dribbling down my chin. "I see," said Anna. She motioned the old man to stand away. "Well, we shall have to see what we can do to help you, Peter. This is most unsatisfactory. You will make yourself ill, and that's not what we want at all. Is it?" She began emptying the contents of two of the sachets in a saucer, adding a little water and mixing up a smooth paste with a spoon. From a cupboard on the wall she took two gauze swabs which she rolled up into pads and soaked in the mixture. She looked impatiently at her watch. Tom was now standing somewhere behind me.

"Right, Tom, ready," she said. He came forward and placed his hands lightly on my shoulders. She came over and put the saucer in my lap. From her bag she took a pen which she used to prize open my lips. "God, those teeth," she said. "Make a mental note, Tom, we must get those seen to." She poked around with her sharp-nailed finger. "Some of these are so loose I could pull them out with my hand. Don't you want to keep your teeth, Peter? You are a silly boy, neglecting yourself so," she said while she took the pads from the saucer and pushed one into each corner of my cheeks.

The first sensation was somewhere in the roof of my head. I could have sworn I was smelling rich flowers or freshly cut vegetation. Then a hot sweet oil began burning into the roots of my jaw and my whole mouth started to hiss and sizzle as though it were frying. My eyes streamed and I became frightened to breathe. I was dribbling badly, from my mouth, my nose, my ears, and I wondered if it was blood. They were burning away the muscle, of that there seemed no doubt, for my chin began to drop. I was about to gulp in cool refreshing air when, on Anna's nodded instruction Tom put his strong hand beneath my jaw and clamped my mouth shut, causing me to bite a corner from my tongue. I could no longer breathe, neither through will nor desire. I could hear the wheels of my chair wriggling somewhere beneath me on the cold stone of the kitchen floor. At last she nodded to Tom and he released his grip. My cheeks suddenly became puffed and a huge flood of liquid poured from the hook of my jaw, into my open mouth and the two pads, yellowed and small, fell out on a bed of saliva. Anna stood upright and wiped the mist from her forehead. "There," she said, a little breathlessly. "You can open your mouth if you want to, can't you Peter? Ready for a drink now? I'll bet you are." She gestured to Tom to wipe my mouth and front, which he did with a tea towel while she went to the fridge and poured a glass of milk. "Right, Peter," she said. "Drink."

She crooked her fingers into the top aspects of the orbits of my eyes and wrenched my head back with an unnecessary violence. She poured the milk into my mouth and I had no choice but to swallow, gobs of air accompanying the icy fluid, making my insides bloat and roll. When she had finished she showed Tom where she was putting the rest of the sachets. He nodded blankly. "And now," she said tartly, "I think you should feed him. And none of that liquidized muck either."

She left the kitchen with the jaunt of a schoolgirl, her heels making hammer taps on the stone floor.

Soon it reached the point where the mere sight of one of those purple sachets dangled before my eyes made my mouth unlock and I would begin unhappily lusting for the odd food Tom brought me, suckling it even though my teeth grated in an unspeakable agony. And the food knifed at my insides and I envisaged whole chunks of stomach, lung and pancreas, being dismembered, rotting, evaporating, being dissipated through my pores, my shit, my breath.

I might have seen their behavior as unreasonable, though I was never one to criticize. Tom, on the other hand, seemed quietly put out at having had to administer this treatment. Maybe he thought it harsh, unethical. If that was the case then he was not alone, for another member of our queer household emerged with the same opinion.

∎ E I G H T ∎

''MONEY. IT HAS to be that. Money at the bottom of everything. Honor? Duty? Professional pride? Not likely. Old hat. Old fashioned. Once maybe, but not now. No. Nothing like the quids to motivate a man, give him reason, aspirations beyond his station, and all that. Prestigious, though, this project. Only been going a couple of years and they've had a ream of publicity. One wonders why, though.''

The Major was wheeling me through the woods. It was a weekend day and there was no work allotted to the house at that time of the week. My own efforts, that is, my therapeutic program, were also eased. No exercises in the gymnasium, no baths, only the bare bones of injection and heavy feeding. John and Anna seemed to take it in turns to go away for the weekend, and this time it was John's turn to remain at the house. Mostly he left people to their own devices, be it staying in bed the whole two days, going out to a nearby town—which he particularly approved of—or simply idling about the house watching sports or films on the television. For his own part he was rarely inclined to leave the smoky comfort of his office. We passed on up a track, down a dark tunnel of overgrowth, the bright sun a jewel moving parallel and as witness at the other side of the deep thicket. In front of us a few tresses of cloud lay snagged on a pure blue sky. The Major seemed in good humour.

"Problems," he said. "They've got problems, I know that. Don't suppose anyone's bothered to tell you what goes on round here. Guinea pigs, that's us. That's you and me, Peter

∎ 42 ∎

my boy. Truth is, I think they're going a bit far these days, overstepping the mark to get results. I heard about what they did to you the other day. Christ, if a man doesn't want to eat, he doesn't want to eat. That stuff they used, illegal now, in fact always has been for humans. Used to use it on cows with some kind of lockjaw or something. Got a brother very big in the pharmaceutical business, he clued me in on that one. I knew Kaufmann, too. They gave him it. Only old Tom got the dose wrong, very nearly blew the fellow's head off, sure to have done some permanent damage to the man. Still, he's gone now and that won't matter. He was a bit like you. You should have met him, maybe you'd have got on together."

He put the brake on the wheelchair and sat on an old log. He was wearing a sort of jacket with no sleeves under which he had only a shirt, yet the cold did not seem to bother him. Or maybe it was me. Not used to it. He took a tin from his pocket and began rolling a cigarette.

"Yeah, guinea pigs," he said. "That's us." He blew smoke onto the chill air. "It doesn't figure," he said. "We're all so different. You'd think if they were going in for this specialized treatment lark they would lump people together who all had the same problems. Here we are, all being boiled up in the same pot, yet we're hardly able to have a decent conversation with one another. Doesn't make sense. Not to me anyhow. Been here six months myself. I'm OK now. Bastards know I've nowhere to go, though. I sometimes think they keep me just for when the inspectors come round. I must look good, presentable or something. They exaggerate everything of course, tell them the worst about me, how sick I was when they brought me here, what stunning progress I've made and all that crap. Truth is, I was never that bad. Bit of trouble with my temper, that's all. The wife cleared off, took the kids. That can't have helped, I suppose. Drank a bit too. But not now. They reckon I half-killed a guy. Daft thing to say: you either kill someone or you don't. Personally I remember nothing. They gave me a drug meant to make me remember but all I saw was ghosts hiding in the grass. They could discharge me now but they won't find me anywhere to live. Bastards. I don't know what they've got planned for you. If I did know, you'd be the first to find out. If I find out I'll tell you. Did the same for Kaufmann. Didn't help him though, didn't stop him going clean out of his mind. They got him out first, clever piece of work. But I could tell he wasn't right. We all could. Time I put pen to paper. There ought to be some sort of investigation into the things that go on round here. One day we'll all end up like Kaufmann. Mind, you're a one, aren't you? I watched them bring you in. You're putting up a bloody good show. I bet no one's ever pulled the wool over your eyes. What's your secret? I've never seen such willpower. Nineteen years in the army, two years in a bin before this place and I've never met one like you before. What's your secret? You can tell me. I'd love to know and I shan't repeat a word to anyone. Go on, Peter. You tell me."

He looked at me, chuckled, then started to cry.

I often wondered what attracted some people to me, what they saw in me. There was a man at the hospital once, someone not dissimilar to the Major, who moaned and wailed a lot of the short time he was in there. He took to taking me for walks in the hospital grounds, long walks, whole afternoons when he would sit on a bench near the bowling green or by the church telling me his problems, reckoning I was the only one who understood. There's no accounting for some people. Anyway, one day he just seemed to decide he was better, took his discharge and, to my knowledge, was never seen in the place again. Cured, I suppose.

The Major sat with his head in his hands, then looked up into the last of the afternoon sun, wiping his cheeks once with his fingertips. "We'd better go," he said, "before the bastards start sending out a search party." He pushed me back through the thicket tunnel where darkness had already collected, even though the ceiling of the sky was yet the same icy blue as before.

When we arrived back at the house there was an air of

mystery about those present. Someone nodded to the Major as we entered the front door. "Oh yes, of course," he said, sounding cheerful again. He wheeled me through to a cloak-room where he went about the awkward procedure of re-moving the coat I had been loaned, taking his time, relieving himself in the toilet, whistling. Then someone, one of the women, popped her head around the door. "All right," she said, "everything's ready." "Good," said the Major and he wheeled me out of the gloomy room into the kitchen where all the residents were assembled together with John and Tom. They brought me forward to a table laden with brightly colored things. In the center was a cake. There was an awk-ward silence before someone cleared his throat and said qui-etly, "Happy birthday, Peter." "Yes," chimed another, "happy birthday, Peter." "Happy birthday," they all said.

Another contrivance, I was certain of that. I could not re-ally believe they had a record of my date of birth; it would all be guesswork. They began chattering nervously. "Cut the cake," called the Major. "Yes, cut the cake," said a triplet. Tom stepped forward and began slicing the yellow thing up. Hands reached for it. "Oh no," he said. "Birthday boy first." He brought me a piece on a silver knife and my mouth flapped crazily in anticipation.

"Thirty-three today," someone called.

I couldn't believe that. I couldn't believe any of them. You never knew what was going to come out next in the kind of company I kept.

NINE

HOW NICE IT would have been to have had some kind of order in my head, to have had my mind sectioned off into compartments, little boxes on the dusty floor of my brain, here my grievances, in this one my fears, here the past, here the dark future. I should have visited each at will, or perhaps I should have left them all tightly locked, keeping the key of course, admiring and fussing over their security, pondering how I might make them even more innocuous. I should never have thrown the key away, that would never have done since I should always have been in deepest fear of someone finding it and undoing my work.

Survival, it has to be said, was my chief, no my single, concern. I worried over my health and the changes being brought about in me. Sometimes I thought I would explode with all the stuff Tom poured down my throat. Anxiety breeds anxiety and sometimes I reentertained one of my oldest fears: that of going blind. And here I give myself away. Oh, I might have claimed I felt I had no influence on those who ministered to me; and yes, I might have believed that I did not care; but I was only flesh and blood, still flesh and blood, just like them. My sight was my life and although unreliable at times it was my distraction from myself for, if left totally to my own devices I should crack, perish, if I were lucky.

Later, a day or two after my "birthday," I enjoyed a short respite from the attentions of John and Anna. Once a week they held some kind of a meeting to which any of the residents might be called to discuss their progress, their personal therapeutic regime, their views on the place—all kinds of things like that. The Major deemed these meetings to be very important but he was rarely called and his own requests for an audience, while being granted, were considered shallow and lost their authenticity in their not being issued from "above." Even I was summoned on one occasion to the dingy office, though the points up for discussion were naturally completely one-sided, and the details were trivial.

After this particular meeting an excitement became apparent in the house. Jackie, one of the residents, had, in John's terms, "achieved social realignment status." That is, she could go home.

Of all the residents at One World she was perhaps the most normal, or the least affected, whichever way you might care to look at it, and as such she was probably the most invisible. A middle-aged, tidy woman she was mild-mannered, shy, and had little to do with me, though I sometimes saw the Major beckon her away to some discussion beyond my earshot. She was mousy, pleasant, not the kind you might expect in a place such as that. She would be leaving the very next day.

We all lined up outside the front door, in the rain, and she hugged people, shook hands, even kissed me on the forehead. The taxi came and she was gone. Where she was destined for exactly, I never knew, people never seemed to think to tell me factual things, just things about themselves and things they seemed to think I should be doing. Wherever it was she was supposed to be going, she never arrived. Instead she went to a canal and drowned herself.

The news returned quickly to One World via a police car and two officers. "Drowned?" whispered one of the triplets standing beside me, cupping her hand to her mouth then drawing her companion away to some place where they might discuss the matter without being overheard. The Major became very tight-lipped for a while, his agitation simmering, an electric charge threading its way inside his long thin body. Even Tom seemed put out, and for a day or two his work lacked conviction.

John and Anna seemed to retreat into themselves for a while. The bed was not filled. A quietness, a chilly sort of respect, descended on the household; nobody seemed to have much to say to anyone else, and if they did say anything it was excessively polite. It was a while before things returned to the way they had been before and the triplets began charging up and down the stairs again, avoiding any place I was since I seemed to frighten or spook them in some way. Not that I was bothered.

Spring was coming. It was around somewhere, blowing in on fresh, sweet air, sparking life off the way it does. The Director of One World and his assistant needed new inspiration and I, though not directly suffering the blame for Jackie's death as I might have done at a not-so-distant previous time, became the target for their further inspiration. Why me? Because I was easy to deal with I suppose. I offered little resistance.

The old exercises were elaborated on. A wooden frame, a machine of sorts, was brought into the gym. It filled the room. I was placed on the seat and straps were drawn across my chest and thighs. Tom then positioned himself behind me and began heaving at the protruding bars and levers. The machine lurched me forward, leaned me back, parted my legs if need be, raising and flexing them in complex, excruciating variation, until I was left spinning and exhausted. This apparatus cost Tom less in terms of effort than before when he had had only his strength to manipulate my increasing weight through a less sophisticated program. The machine creaked and groaned, and more than once a support piece would snap and have to be repaired. I could smell the new wood of which the thing was made; undoubtedly it had been put together in one of the workshops behind the house. Often I wondered, as my head was spun through an arc, my mirrored image crashing toward me then receding, whose hands had been at work in the construction of this odd monster, and, perhaps more importantly, who had dreamed up such a design? Based on what principles?

Tom seemed to take to it with some quiet, if reluctant, enthusiasm, and after one protracted session I felt especially weary. Hot pokers were in my back and neck and my legs were cold, promising pain for the next day. Then I began to feel the exhaustion outside my body: it lay heavy on my cheekbones, played about my head and heels like static, like one enveloping spirit, like many small spirits pirouetting up my spine, tickling, teasing, seeking entry; a racy, rushing feeling, as though all the momentum put into me by that machine was now after release, hesitant at first, reluctant to leave the shell, then all at once pouring out of me, propelling me headlong out of myself—though my body, of course, remained perfectly still. I became dizzy, my focus on things was bubbled, streamed, unreliable. At the evening meal I was given copious amounts of fluid, enriched fruity drinks and milkshakes, no doubt as the result of some proxy decision that the amount of energy I was burning up had to be replaced with enhanced quantities of foodstuffs. My mouth flapped madly, and I slobbered but tolerated the stuff. When everyone else had gone Tom came back for me and told me that instead of my being taken to the lounge as usual he was taking me straight up to bed. I took this to mean that he had somehow noticed my fatigue, for he had become quite adept at anticipating some of my needs.

He said nothing as he wheeled me into my room, indeed he appeared to have dispensed with many of the old formalities in his dealings with me, tired perhaps of talking to himself, feeling a bit silly, at odds with his superiors. Only a day or two before he had emptied the water jug that stood on the table beside my bed, which had been meant for my use but which had only gathered dust. That evening, as if to imply some kind of conspiracy in which he took my part for granted, he put his forefinger to his lips and pointed to the bed. Drawing back the covers he revealed a black pad, about a yard square, underneath the bottom sheet. He carefully replaced the sheet then drew my attention to a flex running from the pad to a small white box hidden behind the bed. A yellow light gleamed beneath a piece of plaster stuck over it to dull the glow. I had prior experience of such devices: when I wet the bed a contact would be made in the pad and a bell would ring in the box to wake me up and alert me to the fact that I was being incontinent. Simple. I had no fear of this contraption. He helped me into the bed.

I listened to the sounds of the house, the television downstairs, the triplets, the Major's laughter, the compulsive drinker in the room next to mine gorging herself with water from the washbasin, her vomit padding softly against the walls and door; then my tiredness overtook me and I slept.

Some time later when the house had gone quiet, dark and cold, I was awake, in anticipation it seemed, of my pissing the bed. I felt the drips oozing, trickling down my balls and onto the sheet. But there was no bell, only a tape recording crackling into life, gently admonishing me, "Dirty Peter. You're not a child."

At first this did not seem so remarkable, just a variation on the bell technique I had encountered before. Then I realized there was more to the device.

The urine stopped dripping from me as I concentrated my attention on the gentle voice whispering to me in the night and the dark, "Lazy Peter. What a to-do. What a messy business. Why disgrace yourself this way? This dirty habit, it's simply not becoming for you. You can do better, don't you think? Come on, try. Think what you're doing, why you're doing it. Think of the trouble it puts other people to. Poor Tom. Poor John. Poor Anna. Selfish Peter."

There was something beyond the words, a little kingdom hidden between their texture. At first it was only faintly familiar, but it quickly made itself apparent to me and I was filled with a nightmarish terror. Was there no end to their ghastly ingenuity? The floodgates between my legs gushed open and my intestines retched horribly, making me shit until I thought I was going to die. Dear God. Dear, dear God. That voice, that warm, killing, woman's voice, belonged to my own mother.

TEN

''SEX. COULD BE sex. Has to be something. Nah. No. Not sex. Their efforts are too strenuous, too sustained for that. You don't keep up a front like that just for sex. Besides, Peter, could you imagine the feline Anna coyly baring her razored pussy for that grease-head? I don't think so. I don't really know, but I don't think so.''

The Major continued pitching stones through the freezing mist, his target a line of bottles at a far edge of the old, wooded quarry he had brought me to. He had lent me a coat, a sheepskin, put it on me himself, then brought me out without seeking permission. I doubted that it would matter.

"They're weird, oddball," he said as he winged a white stone to break the neck of a bottle. The crack rang in the trees, then was muffled in the close gray beyond. "Something," he said, "should be done. There's an authority somewhere. Has to be. Someone to whom they are accountable. Everybody's accountable to someone. They just don't do things right, they overstep the mark. I was better off, better treated where I was before. Bet that applies to you too, eh?"

I was beset by depression, it had lain siege to me, coming in waves day after day, a withering possession that had taken hold and would not let go. Bad times. Sometimes I would ask myself the same questions as the Major: What was in it for them? Where did they find the initiative, this animated desire to take me apart, build me up, reinvent me? I had no satisfactory answer, save the recurrent notion that somehow they were really attempting a reconstruction of their own selves, imposing on me an image of the way they thought they were, or should be. But it was not for me really, this odd philosophizing, moralizing and debating; I had enough on my mind. And I could neither condone nor condemn the Major's sexual theory: I who had never looked with pleasure on any man, woman, or beast. I should have blocked my thoughts altogether, they were dangerous, insoluble, no end to them, best left alone. But the resentment I felt over their incessant interference in my existence, the misery, the despairing idea that there would never be any compromise on their part, led me to brood, thus compounding my hopelessness and faltering faith.

John tended to keep his distance from the residents; it seemed to be his method. I would catch glimpses of him setting off to break the ice on his pond or deposit a new specimen or return with a fresh corpse in an envelope. At mealtimes he would slip into the kitchen when he thought everyone else had gone, to take from the oven the meal which Tom had made him. If I was there he would be taken aback by my unexpected presence and might offer a nod and one of his tight, crooked little smiles in recognition. If he was in a hurry he seemed quite nimble, but there were times when he seemed in some kind of pain, as he shuffled along with the slightest of limps, his footsteps odd on the carpeted, creaking hall floor. I could not fathom him and it would be unwise to try. It would come to no good, do me no good if I tried to slip out of my role of patient, submissive, recipient of his assumedly higher knowledge. I had learned that kind of thing a long time before. I had to behave myself.

Anna was different, younger, and more aptly vital. Her instructions came from him of course, but there was much of her own dynamism in her work. Perhaps, and obviously, she planned one day to have the One World Rehabilitation Center to herself, and she may well have been in training for that very, suspect, honor, though she was patient and tactful and did nothing to usurp John's place or show disrespect for his wishes. Much of the program they inflicted was, I believed, of her own original design. The tapes, for instance, which lullabied on into the night, sometimes different, often the same repetitive ten sentences, ten minutes, I don't know how long they were—those could well have been all her own idea, for the voice that cajoled and whispered from behind my bed was certainly hers, artistically disguised of course, but most certainly hers. My mother was dead, had been for many years, I came to remember—as I came to remember many things, new baubles rising from the swamp, crashing from the ceiling, no stopping them. Bad times.

Soon, however, I began genuinely to tire of the tapes, and once I saw how harmless they were I was able to disregard them altogether. I did wonder, though, how many of the other residents, perhaps of less fibrous will than myself, might have been subjected to some similar treatment, the content of the dialogue tailored to each particular case, more intense maybe, harrowing enough to drive some poor soul out of his mind.

The Major stalked around the quarry, cursing in the undergrowth, eventually reemerging somewhere above me on a chalk mound down which he slid, scattering shale into the spokes of my wheelchair. "Come on, out of it," he said brightly. "Time we weren't here."

Late in the afternoon Tom wheeled me into the kitchen to give me a haircut. A transistor radio on the window ledge gave out sporadic football results together with garbled commentaries on some of the games. Tom put a towel round my shoulders. "Right, sir," he said cheerfully. "Short back and sides, is it? Or is sir in the mood for something a bit more fancy, more modern? I have no catalog, my good man, but if you were to indicate something of what you had in mind I will do my best to accommodate you. Sorry, Peter," he said, lightly embracing me. "A little joke you understand. Just old Tom playing the fool. Now then, where should we begin?"

He snipped away peacefully. "Used to do this all the time at a place I was in. Maybe you'd know it. Cook Hall? Yes? No? Closed down now. Yes, used to do all the lads' hair, two bob a time. Couldn't do it now, of course. They'd stop my pay or benefit or something." He combed briskly, whistling to himself. Then he stopped, slowly drawing himself upright. "Needed doing, don't you think?" he said, addressing not me but a new presence in the kitchen—John.

"Yes," said John. "Great improvement, Peter."

A ponderous silence fell between the three of us. Finally John spoke.

"I wonder, Tom, if you might leave Peter and me alone for a few minutes? There's something we'd like to discuss."

"Yes, surely," said Tom. He left immediately.

"Peter," John said softly, kneeling at my side, "I've just had the Major in my office. He seems most distressed, and I'm damned if I can find out what the matter is. I understand you and he went for a little walk this afternoon, as you have been doing on a number of occasions, not that there is anything wrong with that, on the contrary, it is to be welcomed that you should be able to get out and about with your fellow residents, fresh air, company, and all that. No, I have not come about that, though I might suggest you pick your friends carefully. You see, Peter, the Major is a highly volatile man, he has his problems. Naturally, you must be thinking, or why else would he be here? He worries, you see; he is sometimes given to thinking that people have it in for him, are conspiring against him in some way. He seems to think, Peter," he paused as if seeking the right words, "he seems to think that you may be plotting to kill him."

He stood up, made an empty gesture with his hands then shuffled off behind me.

The minutes of silence passed. I thought he must have left the room. Then he coughed from somewhere behind me, by the sink maybe.

"Preposterous, isn't it?" he said. "What must be going on in the poor man's mind? How could he think that you, an unmoving, dumb, no, not that, forgive me, you an unspeaking, utterly enigmatic man could possibly be planning to murder someone? It would be laughable if it were not so serious. We should not ridicule the Major. He is suffering from severe mental disturbance, it is his illness, not his fault. But it isn't the Major I am particularly worried about at this moment. He will recover. Tomorrow he will deny all knowledge of his accusation, if he is not already doing so. What I must say, knowing the Major and his condition with such intimacy and depth, what seems remarkable is the fact that it is unusual for him to get so upset without the aid of some precipitating, external factor. Do you see what I'm getting at, Peter?"

I heard him shuffle forward and felt his hands rest on my shoulders. I could smell his sweat as he leaned forward and spoke softly into my ear.

"I have to know, Peter. When you were out with the Major this afternoon, did you speak to him? Please feel at ease. I should like it if you now decided to be frank with me, come clean as it were. Nothing would be held against you. And you are coming out of yourself, we have seen that. Now would be as good a time as any. What did you say to him, Peter? You did say something to him, didn't you? He hinted as much. Come on, Peter, open your mouth. Tell me. Speak to me."

He was now embracing me, nuzzling his mouth and nose in my neck and hair. He cuddled me tight, pleading quietly, "Tell me dear boy. Tell me, your friend, the things he wants to know."

I wondered if he was weeping. Then I realized that the noise he was making, burbling into my collar, was a giggle, a salivary, nasal laugh. He straightened himself up behind me and patted me lightly on the shoulders.

"So you won't say anything to me, then, Peter?" he asked as he came round in front of me. "No. No, of course not. It's hardly your style. God, but you're a cunning bastard. A cunning bastard and no mistake."

He laughed out loud, then turned and left the kitchen.

. E L E V E N .

FOOD FOR MY compliance, a straight exchange—that seemed to be the deal, that is what the dream promised. I might have been in the house, it felt like I was, but I was elsewhere, had to be since I could see an image of the house and its attentive features through a window, a window of the place I was in, a familiar room, a cell, though I could never say for sure. Anna and Tom were there, happy, a festiveness about them. Outside there was a clanking and hammering—a gallows being built? No. Something else, more elaborate, though its purpose would be the same, namely my own execution. Tom stirred a yellow pulp in a big drum. Anna took a lump in her hand and offered it to me, pressing it against my cheek, pushing her wet finger into my mouth. Tom was indifferent, bored. He went to look out of the window at a mass of water in which floated expressionless heads and odd bodies. The water was rising, threatening to engulf us all. He looked on impassively. I wondered if I were dead. Anna walked round on her hands, skirts falling over her face. She fell to the ground laughing, rolling over to scoop up my wheelchair and send me sprawling. Others were present, I don't know who. I was put on a toilet, my legs spread, my ass a wide cavern from which Anna dragged long, skin-coloured turds which turned to wriggling reptiles in her hands. These she put before my face.

I lay in the dark, my eyes open, my head still full of the images of that dream, all haphazard, chronologically lapsed. I sought clearer pictures, looked for meanings that would be palatable to me. Eventually there was nothing, only a stain on my memory, indistinguishable.

The machine behind my head was quiet. It might have spoken in my sleep, but I had not heard it. The room was cold and all I could see was the door, black against the purple and silver of the wall, a tombstone set against an unpeopled land beneath a godless sky. From somewhere came a snore, a plaintive mumbling, someone else dreaming in this house of dreams, this place of inhuman alliances. The wardrobe cracked, cracked again, then was silent. I could feel no heartbeat. Cold air lingered over my mouth, unused, uninvited. The blood was still in my veins, my flat, unexcited veins. The juices in my body were soured, heavy, needing the light. I could think of nothing, I was nothing, nothing alighting in nothingness, a dream of myself, no more. Not even that.

TWELVE

ANOTHER DAY.

My sense of time is and was always bad. I had no idea how long I had been at One World, many weeks, some months certainly. I would now be forgotten back at the hospital. My bed there, although officially classed as a leave bed, would be occupied by someone else, someone new, and might well have been filled the very afternoon of my departure, such was the way of things in that unlikely haven.

Tom strode into my room and lifted the window wide open. The skies outside were fine and airy and this seemed to lift him as he went about the tedious business of dressing me and shaving me with the electric razor, which he did with particular care, bathing my face afterwards and patting it dry with a warm towel. I often wondered where he slept; it was somewhere on the premises for he was certainly in attendance twenty-four hours a day, unlike John and Anna who left their cars at the front of the house in full view of anyone who might wish to monitor their comings and goings. Tom would be in some quarter, away from the residents as might befit someone who was no longer a resident but a member of staff. There were many parts of the house to which I was not offered or allowed access.

He eased me into the chair and pushed me out along the landing. He stopped at the top of the stairs to knock on the last of a row of brown-painted doors.

In this room slept the man who pulled out his hair, Murray I think his name was, or perhaps it was something else, it is of no real consequence. He was a small, deferential man who normally rose without prompting, who liked his own company best of all. Tom found him hanging at the back of the door, a noose of finely plaited human hair drawn tight around his neck. Inside the room I could see more of the stuff, hair falling in brown clouds from open drawers, piled on the bed like a sleeping bear, ankle deep about the floor. A warm, animal smell came from the darkened room, not unpleasant. Tom gawped and shocked himself into action, slamming the door on me, grunting as he took the weight of the man and lifted him down and onto the hairy bed. He opened the door, his abiding happy mood apparently dented though not, I suspected, completely destroyed, for despite the horror of his discovery he was an old man and as one gets older it becomes difficult simply to jump from one emotion to another, whatever the circumstances. He was also a hardened man, like myself, and he had probably seen dozens of such sights during the course of his career as a psychiatric patient. The best he could manage before running off down the stairs was to say, "I wish you would do something useful instead of sitting in that fucking chair all day."

I was left facing the man I thought might be called Murray. He lay on the bed, a moment of surprise caught on his face for all eternity, the hair rope twisting from his neck like an umbilical cord, like a snake which had met its own end in finishing off Murray. And it was a bad place for me to be, bad for me to witness such a thing, that black tongue pointing at me, accusing, saying, "Your fault, Your fault." I would be getting a reputation for being around at the scene of people's suicides. They would be saying I brought bad luck.

This incident gave all the residents a free morning. The Major was commandeered by Tom to "see to him." He took me into the lounge where he read a newspaper and said nothing. Later he wheeled me outside under the shade of the trees at the side of the house from where we could see John, Anna, Tom, and a policeman supervising the removal of the body into an ambulance. The vehicle's radio crackled and the faint smell of its disinfected interior radiated across to us on the light breath of the warm wind. "Cold-blooded murder. Killers, every one of them," said the Major, his muttered words falling on the top of my head. Without actually having appeared to see us, John limped away from the departing ambulance in our direction. His face was dark and greasy, his tie askew. He showed his yellow teeth. "Get him away from here," he hissed.

In an act of blunt recalcitrance the Major took me back to the house, lifted me from the wheelchair at the foot of the stairs and carried me, slung over his back, to my room where he laid me on the bed beneath the open window. This, of course, suited me admirably, though I feared I might suffer later. The house could go about its own agitation and depressions without me, beneath me in the rooms below, and I would have to partake of none of it. The air flowing over me was rich, succulent, and to my subsequent surprise I began dozing, so relaxed did I feel—though that was probably just a frame of mind, a reaction from the relief of not having to perform those foolish exercises.

When I awoke I heard a new noise, a ferreting, scratchy sound, very close, somewhere in the room. A bird? Was it from somewhere closer still, from inside my own body? A tearing of my component parts? No. A terror was upon me worse even than the momentary fear I felt that I was breaking up inside. A flush of sweat prickled in my hair: I had located the sound. It was under the blanket the Major had thrown over me, at a far corner of the bed, a rising and falling: my foot was moving.

There was no hiding it. Over the pink dunes of my cheeks I could see the foot, its staccato lifting and jerking moving the blanket away, my toes wet and warm, the heel tapping into the mattress, a light playful movement like a faltering pulse. I bent my will towards it, trying in vain to halt it, weeping inside over the fact that I was losing control of myself. Hours passed. Tom came.

He noticed it immediately, seemed almost to anticipate it.

He examined me minutely for any further signs of movement, lifting my other leg and letting it fall, pressing the
moving one down to try and make it stop. He was unsuccessful. He looked deep into my eyes, his own full of sobriety
and reserve. Then he went for John and Anna.

The Director of the One World Intensive Rehabilitation
Center grinned. "And what do we call this?" he asked of the
other two. He clamped my ankle down with his thick heavy
hand and I could feel the impulse working against his grip,
throbbing the length of my leg. He quickly drew his hand
away and my leg bounced off the bed before resuming its
previous light momentum.

"He's not trying to communicate with us, by any chance?"
asked Anna.

"I don't know," said John. "It could be a trapped nerve.
We should have it investigated but then again . . ." he
paused. "Perhaps," he said, "perhaps we might subscribe to
the theory that he is trying to tell us something. Maybe we've
reached a milestone, broken through somewhere. I wish he
would say something, I've always been convinced that the
vocal cords are intact, and yet nothing, not a murmur. Tell
me, Peter, come on old man, say something. Say. Say."

He breathed deeply, smiling.

"We'll take it as a sign. Have to. There may never be
another opportunity like it," he said. "Tom, you know the
procedure for inducing anamnesis, nothing to eat or drink for
the next twelve hours. Understood?"

Tom nodded, though his face was a picture of reluctance.

"Right Peter," said John. "I want you to listen to me very
carefully. And I know you can hear me and can understand
what I'm saying. We're sending you on a little journey back
to where you came from, to a life you once knew, to the
times which made you as you are now. Nothing to be afraid
of; on the contrary, we are in the business of relieving pain
and suffering and that is how you should see this opportunity,
this chance to go back to the beginning and make amends.
You are privileged to be receiving this service, and I hope

you will respond with the same grace as we are according you by snapping out of yourself, back in to the real world, the one world that is life for all of us."

Tom lingered, when the other two had gone, looking down at my foot, puzzled, concerned, seeming to need to explain something to me. He covered me over with the blanket and left the room.

Once more it appeared I was being made to pay for someone else's misfortune. Could any of it really have been my fault? Wasn't I being brought to task just a little too often? Being held responsible for the madness around me, tried and convicted without anyone to say a word in my defense, could that be right? I don't know. Nor did I really understand what was going to happen to me, though it was not long before I found out.

They came in the early hours of the next morning, John and Tom, lifting me down the stairs and away into the cellar with the stealth of anxious murderers. This, I thought, really is the end. Now I was to be disposed of, dismembered perhaps, my pieces atomized and fed to the boiler or scattered in the woodland. The cellar was a suitable place, homely in a perverse sort of way with its sooty brick walls, a square of dawn light at one end boosted by the light bulb dangling from the ceiling, a pile of coke near a room which I guessed housed the boiler, a close, warm, barren smell, old air—this would do, I thought in my misery. I would be happy to go now.

Tom took hold of me, hugging me from behind, his customary strong grip squeezing at my innards, mulching them, turning them to soup. I became limp and fell forward but he countered this by crushing me tighter still, lifting me clear of the floor, my leg flapping crazily, banging his shins. John went over to the wall and began fiddling with a set of ropes and pulleys. From the shadows an ungainly framework suspended by an intricate interweaving of ropes descended before us, rocking downwards till it was about knee-height above the floor. Tom shuffled me across and the two of them laid me on the frame, John stretching my arms out at my side. From a sack he produced pieces of canvas which he wrapped about my arms and legs, looping them underneath the frame, securing them with zips and laces. Both he and Tom found their work hard going and John stood back to give himself a rest and to ponder my position. He made minor adjustments to the fastenings. "Right," he said at last, and the two of them went over to the wall and began hauling on the ropes in unison.

I found myself being raised, feet uppermost, before the apparatus suddenly groaned and twisted, and I was suspended looking at the floor, hovering like a bird, like someone frozen in the act of throwing himself from a height. Tom nudged a crate across the floor with his foot while John secured the hauling system. At a nod from John the old man produced a cotton bag, a hood which he placed over my head and drew lightly about my neck with a cord. I felt a needle in my arm then heard the door close as they left.

I was alone in the blackness, hanging weightless, my face wet with the condensation from my breath and from my sweat, since I too had felt the exertion involved in this effort. There was terror too, hidden somewhere in some hole, in some dark abyss in my mind. My heart, that dry old vessel, began stabbing rustily, surging into life—surely some part of it would rupture, some chamber split open with the pressure, spilling the bile it carried to poison what remained of the rest of my insides? I began to see pools of color in the darkness, spreading like oil on water. I was choking, sure to be. I began to see old shapes, hear ancient voices laughing in the shadowlands of my recall. Thus, it seemed, I was to be destroyed, I balked at my thoughts, ducking and feinting, but there was no escape. In an instant I realized the purpose of this new game: I was being asked to confront my past, my history. It would render me senseless, of that I felt sure. I began to see old forgotten images, not so much visually as by inference, pictures so powerfully suggested that I felt I had already passed beyond the point of death and was now keeping company with ghosts who had joyfully come to claim me as one of their own.

· T H I R T E E N ·

MY SISTER, ALISON, if that was her name, yes, that was her name, led me by the hand to a clearing she had made in our weed-strewn back garden, her long white fingers wrapped firmly about my wrist. Maybe she was eleven or twelve years old then, I don't know, a bit older than me, I think. "You can sit there," she said, pointing to a corner of the old rug she had brought from the kitchen and laid in the green overgrowth. I sat down.

She was wearing shorts, a yellow vest, and a pair of our mother's sunglasses which were black and covered half her face. When she saw that I had sat down she lay on her back in the thundery warmth, looking at the skies for a few moments. She sat up, snatching an old magazine from the untidy pile at her side, magazines given to her by a girlfriend a long time ago. She flicked the pages over irritably then stopped to read for a while. "Oh my God," she said. "Oh my dear God, the things they put in here. Rubbish. For kids. 'Hazel eyes,' 'Dreamboats,' it's enough to make you puke." She threw the magazine aside and stood up, kicking off her sandals. She knelt beside me. "Do you know what I'd do," she said, "if my 'Dreamboat' lover came along right now, right this very minute?" She leaned closer, whispering, her lemon breath on my cheek. "Do you know what I would do, my little quiet one?" She lay on her back again, her legs flat on the rug, her toes twitching. "I'd do this," she said, "sit back just like this. Then I'd let him have his whole rotten evil way with me. And afterwards . . ." She paused, cupping her hand over her mouth, her soft yellow stomach quivering with suppressed laughter. "Afterwards," she said, "before he went on his way again, he might condescend to toss me a nice bright shiny coin." She laughed forcibly, rolling on to her side, her long straight hair falling over her face.

Thunder rumbled from somewhere over the fields at the back of the estate where we lived. A woman appeared in the next garden to bring in washing from her line. She stared at us, her hands on her hips. Alison sat up and returned her stare, making a screeching noise then flopping back to the dirty wool of the rug, her arms and legs tremulous, crooking slowly into the shape of a human swastika, her tongue lolling, her eyes strained to show the whites. She remained motionless, unbreathing. The woman stepped up to the fence. "Is she all right? Your sister? What's the matter with her?" Alison suddenly jumped up, dancing and kicking. "No," said my sister, "I'm not all right. I'm a loony, you know that. We're all loonies here, that's what you all say, isn't it?" She fell into the grass, then crawled up to where I sat, sobbing now, resting her head on my crossed leg. The woman tutted. "You're not all there, you lot. There should be somewhere for people like you." She went into her house and began arguing loudly with someone inside.

We, that is me, Alison, our mother and father, lived at the end of a village, near a big town, in a maze of red-bricked, red-roofed houses, all like our own, grouped in twos and fours around rough greens, looking at each other. It was somewhere, I don't know where, a "North of England," a "Yorkshire," which could have been the land to the end of the field behind our house or it could have extended to the very extremities of finite life; it was a place or it was an idea or it was a people, I could never decide which.

When I was very small, since I did not speak, I was sent to a special school with other children who had slit eyes and hard flat heads. They could be very wild and they did mad things, biting their fingers to the bone then gnawing the bone itself if they could get away with it, fighting as if possessed, baby minds in growing children's bodies. Some wore leather pads strapped to their heads to protect them when they threw themselves to the hard concrete of the high-fenced playground. It wasn't so bad there, though they soon realized I was not like the rest of them and although I think they might have liked to have kept me on account of the fact that I was so quiet, I was eventually taken away to a children's ward annexed to some hospital, I don't know where. There I learned to read and write, that kind of thing; they said I could be quite bright. I would go home at weekends and for long leaves, until I hardly seemed to need to be in a hospital at all and I was taken away and sent to the same school as Alison. That's when I started having the fits, jackknifing from my seat and thrashing away on the classroom floor, no air, biting holes in my tongue, a body fighting alone—they say you're not meant to remember what happens to you during a fit, but I can recall everything, the throb to my temples, the taste of blood in my mouth, the curious looks of my classmates as they gathered around me, and the mixed skepticism and fear on the face of the teacher as she knelt beside me. I was put back on the children's ward.

The people on the estate talked about me often; I did not imagine this, since my sense of hearing was and has always been very good. Sometimes I would go to the shop for my father and I began to realize how artificially cheerful the woman behind the counter was, counting my change into my palm unnecessarily loudly and methodically. The men strolling down the street always avoided my eyes. And when I came home on leave, the news of my return seemed to percolate from house to house with the silly rejoinders those people seemed to go in for, "Shame. Shame for his family. Oh such a shame." Sometimes I got beaten up by other boys, older girls too, and my mother would look at my cut and bloodied face and weep in her detached way.

My mother was tall and very white-skinned. Her hair was long and dark, strayed with white, and she kept it tied back in a rough ponytail tied with funny spotted ribbons. She seemed to take pleasure in small things, things my father and sister might have regarded as merely incidental to their lives: the kitchen with its yellowing wall-cupboards, the tea caddy with the purple lady on the lid, old mugs and cups hanging from badly spaced hooks, the biscuit tin under the sink where she kept dusters and shoe polish. Now and again she might spend her evenings writing, if the mood was on her, poetry mostly, filling shiny-backed exercise books, sitting at the dining table in our parlor. This activity both excited and irritated my father to the point where he would snatch the book from under her pencil and read aloud to Alison and myself commenting, "What good's that, then? I'll tell you, it's no good. Do you know why? Because it doesn't say anything." Alison would become annoyed. "Shush you, nasty," she would say. "Why can't you do anything creative? Why do you have to pull everyone to pieces all the time?" "Do I?" he would counter. "Tell them, Peter, when did I last pull you to pieces? Anyway," he would say, "what's the point in encouraging all this writing stuff if the truth is that she's no good at it? She has no real talent. She'll only look silly in the end, silly like she does now. Nobody would ever want to buy that stuff, so what's the point?" My mother, vapid though I'm sure equal to the task of reprisal against my father, would gently ask for her book back and my father, suddenly and sheepishly, would comply. Later, the next day maybe, I might find my mother crying in her stooped-up, introspective sort of way, the way she did when I came home bruised and bleeding, and I would feel sort of sorry for her, bending over her, puzzling as to where I should put my hands to offer her comfort.

My father was a thin, enigmatic man with a calamitous passion for projects beyond his capabilities, antiques, mushroom farming, sifting for gold dust in the local river, car mechanics even though he could not drive. Mostly he did odd jobs for people on the estate to add to the money he collected from the post office every week. I do not believe we were unhappy, that I must say, though it did seem to me we were never a family given to talking much with each other, not in the way I imagined others might.

One day when I came home on leave Alison took me straight up to her room. Her hair was pinned to one side with a small flower. She was wearing a little woolly cap and silky clothes I had never seen before. She had a cigarette, which she lit. She sat me on her bed and began pacing the floor in front of me. "Peter," she said, "there is something I have to tell you. It is my duty. I must tell you because no one else in this squalid little household would ever think to tell you and I am, after all, your sister and your elder." She drew on the cigarette and sneezed a little as the smoke came out of her nose. "For some time now I have been keeping an eye on Father. In fact, yesterday I felt it necessary to miss school and follow him down into the village. You won't know about his present daft scheme, of course. Mother, that poor suffering woman, thinks it's market gardening, but I have reason to believe that it's something else, something altogether more sinister. You need to know, we both need to know, since it could have implications for us all." She paused, looked out of the window, then into the dressing table mirror, as a result of which she began furiously rubbing at a smear of eye shadow that had run down her cheek. She tilted her head to one side and began her ruminative pacing of the floor again. "Drugs, Peter," she said. "Our father is dealing in drugs. Or it may be guns. Drugs, guns—whatever it is, I fear the inevitable has now happened, that is, our father has descended to the level of the criminal classes. I have seen him with the commonest people. Oh I'm so sorry," she said, throwing herself down in front of me, bracing herself against my knees. "I know," she said, "that all this must come as a shock to you, but you had to know, it is your right. You must promise me, Peter, that you will not let yourself get too upset. We have to be brave and realize that our future happiness cannot be taken for granted any more. Ah life," she said. "Cruel, cruel life."

She stood up, put out the cigarette and went to the window, brushing her hair out of her eyes and folding her arms. She looked out over the fields saying:

"Just once Peter, just one time, I wish you would say something to me."

· FOURTEEN ·

IT WAS LIKE Alison to dramatize things, it was in keeping with the whimsicality of her family. We were an odd bunch, I knew that; I, probably the oddest of them all.

Sometimes my father would get sick, always in the same way, something to do with the skin on his back. It would come upon him in a matter of hours, tedious in its quality and regularity. I might suggest that it was one of the few constant values in his mercurial existence. In keeping with his nature, he would scream his disregard for the illness or else he would take to his bed and declare he was dead and in a state of transition from this life to the ascension into eternity. Once, after an attack which seemed quite momentous, Alison made me stand outside his bedroom door while she crept in to take a folder of photographs from the wardrobe. She was very good at that sort of thing, and my father never stirred from his troubled sleep. She led me out to the garden shed and emptied the snaps on to the floor between us. "This one will do," she said. "No, that's no good, he's too happy on that. This one reflects his personality better. I don't know, though. Here, you shall have that one of you and him." She handed me a small black-and-white print of him carrying me on his shoulders. I was wearing a cloth hat with cartoon characters on it. "I shall have this one," she said, not letting me see. "You do understand, don't you, Peter?" I did not, but the general impression she gave me was that we were to carry these pictures in some kind of memory of our father who was not yet dead. I told you we were odd. My mother later found mine in my trouser pocket, long after Father had recovered, and she thought about it for a while, gave a little smile, and hugged me tight. All without explanation. I digress perhaps.

However elaborate Alison's interpretation of Father's recent behavior had been, there was some truth behind it; that is, he was in some kind of trouble which was to necessitate our moving away from the village very quickly one night in a big wagon, in keeping with Father's incongruous sense of adventure. Mother was dumb the whole way.

Was it at this point that I became unhinged, cast loose in the doubtful precincts of my mind? It would be easy to weld this my story, my confession, as I have said my last, I hope, into an explanation of my later utter intransigence: it was what they wanted with their needles and their blindfolds. But I could not be swayed so easily. It was there, sure enough, my history, a calamity of baubles, something to appease my tormentors' appetites for motive, for cause and effect, neither of which have I genuinely seen to exist. So what? Here, have it anyway.

Somebody, a relative maybe, drove us through the night, huddled in the cab of the wagon, to the coast somewhere in this Yorkshire. We were bumped and jostled in the rickety vehicle along a rough track. I could smell the sea, hear its soft waves, something at once soothing and alarming to me. It was getting light and we were all tired except Alison, whose excitement, inflamed by our father's unaccounted-for euphoria, served to put Mother into a state of silent irritation. We arrived at a small, rundown cottage near the edge of the low cliffs. I stepped from the cab behind my father and went and stood on the springy turf of the cliff top, drawn by the emptiness in front of me, frightened by its hugeness, knowing somewhere in my young mind that this vacuum could suck me out of myself, draw me head, skin and gizzards into a void I could not bear the thought of.

Behind me, the man helped Father and Mother unload our sticks of furniture, shaking his head as Father broke a window at the back of the cottage to get in.

Along the cliff top we were to find other bungalows and houses, empty shops, odd bits of a partly developed tourist village that had failed to catch on, a place of dead dreams, a silly kingdom that immediately captured my father's brittle imagination. "I will work in this place," he said, "and we shall be rich." The air, he also said, would be good for Mother whose nerves had been bad of late. She was indifferent to the move; no, she was passively against it, suffering quietly, knowing it was hopeless to try and argue with her capricious husband. She sat in the kitchen looking back along the cliff top road for many hours, thinking I did not know what.

Within a week of our arrival our neighbors, whoever they were, moved out of the next cottage. Days afterwards an old man who died was taken away by a solitary hearse which my Mother watched bobbing away along the road, turning inland and out of sight. Men came in a truck to board his home up, but this did not stop Alison from breaking in while I stood outside. She came out with a roll of clothes in her arms which she dumped in front of me. "Look what I've found," she said. "You'll never believe, it's so awful." She unrolled what I took to be the dead man's jacket and revealed the furry body of a cat, something black oozing in a bubble from its mouth. "The poor thing," she said. "The poor, poor thing. Of course, we are responsible for it now, aren't we, Peter? We could bury it, but I think we should consider the possibility of disease. It'll have to be cremation."

She left me with the cat while she went to our own cottage, quickly returning with a handful of matches and bits of crushed newspaper which she would have taken from the boxes of Mother's still-unopened crockery and ornaments. "Come on," she said, "nothing to be afraid of. Think of it as our duty." She rewrapped the cat, picked it up and led me off to a copse a little way up from a rift in the cliff. "Here," she said, "this will do. It's nice and sheltered. Appropriate, don't you think?" she said as she began making the newspaper into a pile. She soon realized she had nowhere near enough material and she began searching around for dried grass, leaves and twigs. Eventually she decided: "It is ready." She produced the cat from the bundle and laid it on top of the unlit bonfire. My heart was throbbing, I don't know why. Alison dragged bits of grass from under the cat to obscure its body before she struck a match on a flat stone and lit the paper and the driest of the grass. She took me by the hand and bade me stand back as the flames grew about the little monument. Inexplicably I loosed myself from her grip and ran a few paces up out of the hollow, stopping then and turning to watch the flames reach and crackle. Alison seemed oblivious of my presence as she stepped forward and prodded the fire with a stick to let air into the center. She turned to me, looking in my direction yet appearing to focus some way beyond me. "I should say a prayer," she said, "but I can't think of one. I know, I'll sing instead. The school song, that will do." She began with the words "Land of our birth we pledge to thee . . ." then started to giggle and could not continue the verse. She ran right up to the fire, squealing with curiosity, prodding at the charring, falling outer tent of sticks with her foot, her eager eyes seeking a better view of the cat's smouldering red outline. Then her enthusiasm began to fail as she circled the dying fire and realized that the heat it had given was not strong enough to reduce the cat's bones to ashes. The fire went out and Alison kicked at the little black skeleton. I saw the soft charred entrails nestling in its head and ribcage, and was appalled. My sister ran up the banking, grabbed my hand and led me off, running at first then slowing to a walk as we came to the beach.

The spectacle of the cat weighed heavily on my mind; everything weighed on my mind. I began to examine my own thin constitution, my flesh, my hard fingernails, my soft, white belly, and I took to looking at myself in mirrors, asking myself strange, obscure mental questions, straining backwards to look over my shoulder at the reflection of my thin white back. I would feel my hair, sketch round the features on my face with my thumb, watch the little pulsing vein in my ankle. That this skin, these bones, eyes, teeth, organs, would also one day end up as ashes, as nothing, imparted in me a dread I had not known before. I had an impulse to end my life there and then. I had no experience of suicide, I believed it to be my own invention, and as such it became suspect in my mind. It would never do, I realized that. I hesitated and the urge withered, and became locked and lost somewhere inside me.

What I really wanted was mastery, complete control over my fate, though I had not the vaguest idea of how I was to achieve it. For the moment it became just a heavy notion, more lasting than the phase of suicidal ideas, a silent wilfulness spreading, drying me out, looking for a reason to take me over.

· F I F T E E N ·

ONE DAY MY mother disappeared, simply took herself off without telling anyone. Father sat at the kitchen table with his head in his hands saying, "What's got into her? What have I done?" Alison took some coins from the pocket of the coat hanging on the back of his chair and went to a telephone somewhere. She returned about an hour later saying, "Our mother, your wife, has gone home to see the doctor and I don't blame her. He says she's got to go into hospital for a good rest. What do you say to that?" "Is that so?" said Father, suddenly brightening. "I wonder what those places are really like these days."

The fleshy air of that summer turned thin and sharp. Father did not seem inclined to make my sister and me go to school saying at one point that he would educate us himself, though nothing ever came of that. However, following Mother's departure from our midst Alison became more serious, more central in her young self, and she insisted that Father enroll her in a school she had found out about in some nearby hamlet. "Peter should go too," she said. "I have other plans for Peter," said Father, vaguely trying to restate his position as head of the household. "Besides," he said, "why should he go? He doesn't want to. If he could say I'll bet he would tell us he doesn't want to go to any school." Alison sniffed and frowned.

With winter beginning to snap in the big skies Father became oddly rejuvenated, announcing his plan to adopt the squatters' rights he had used in procuring the cottage to take over one of the empty shops. His idea was to turn it into a seafood restaurant to which, he said, the whole county would flock. My sister was briefly caught up in his euphoria and she clambered over him, egging him on, trailing him for more details. "Peter," said my father, "will wear a frilly-fronted shirt and wait on the tables." "What good will he be?" said Alison. "He'll be our dumb waiter," said Father, his stomach rutting unusually, the way it always did when he found himself amusing. Alison cooled immediately and took me outside to play.

Father did indeed break into one of the shops, one day when Alison was out at school. "You could come down and help," he said to me, but I was not inclined to bother and he did nothing to make me. I often noted that he seemed uneasy when he was alone with me, almost respectful in a funny sort of way. By mistake I did wander down there one morning. He was inside mopping rainwater from behind a door. I peered through the window, and he began making a show of wiping down a counter, taking a handkerchief from his pocket and patting his brow, pretending it was hard work. I moved on down the wind-whipped ghostly street.

At weekends Alison took to going back to our old place, staying with some relative of ours whom I do not remember or probably never even knew. Father too would vanish, often for days at a time. The restaurant idea was, of course, quickly abandoned. He would go to some town, some resort up the coast, to collect his money from the post office. On these trips he would drink himself into some kind of oblivion, though he was usually sober by the time he got back, arms full of groceries, much of it faddy rubbish that we never ate. Occasionally he was remorseful for something or other and I would listen to him ranting through the night while I tried to sleep in my little room, looking at the peeling wallpaper rainbowed with damp. Sometimes I fancied that he wanted me to forgive him for something, though I never knew what.

With so much time available it would have been normal, I suppose, for a boy of my age to go exploring the empty beaches and the coves Alison said existed somewhere, but I rarely went beyond the confines of the cottage and its garden which was slipping into the sea. Sometimes I would wander onto the beach to collect wood, the way Alison had shown me, for the fire, but I was not strong and could only carry pitifully small amounts at a time. If I could stir myself to make a fire I would sit in the room that served as our lounge, staring into the grate, hypnotized by the flames, keeping perfectly still, careless of the hours, forgetting to eat. At other times I might stand in a shaded corner of the kitchen watching out of the window as yet one more removal van came to empty a bungalow along the cliff. I would stand and wait until the occupants turned out the lights and locked the door. Then I might have to move round a little to see the van as it rocked away along the potholed road into the darkening afternoon, leaving no trace as it rolled behind the horizon. Gone. Gone where? I might have asked myself. Gone nowhere. Displaced, that was all. I should have broken into the empty houses; it seemed the thing to do. But I didn't.

One day Alison came back from visiting Mother in the hospital. She sat on the settee, her leg tucked underneath her, idly toying with the stuffing oozing out of our poor furniture. She examined the nails of her hands, then broke into tears, a fearful wailing that seemed to possess her and shape her larger than her years. Father looked at her blankly. "For God's sake," she said. "Can't you ask me what the matter is?" "All right then," he said, "what's the matter with you?" Alison wiped her nose and said, "Mother's cut her wrists." Father stood and put his hands in his pockets. "Is she dead, then?" he asked. "No. No, she's all right." "How," he asked, "could they let her do such a thing?" There was a genuine plaintiveness in his voice and he actually had some moisture in his eyes. "Anyway," he said after a silence, "if she really wanted to do herself in that's not the way to do it. Hardly ever works. She can't have been serious otherwise she would have gone for the throat, here where the arteries are prominent. Or here at the back of the neck." He tapped the place with two closed fingers. "Or the liver, that's a great blood-filled organ. If she went deep enough, that is." Alison wept horribly.

Late into that evening, when Father had gone out to wherever he went, Alison emerged at the door of the lounge where I was with one of Mother's suitcases packed with her own things. She kissed me, said none of it was my fault, and handed me a note which I was to give to Father. When he read it the next day he screwed it up and threw it in the fire without a word.

As winter deepened the storms became very rough, the sea being driven right up under the cliff. The cottages at the edge began to suffer as the water took the earth away with it. Whole rooms fell away at stroke, decorated walls and fireplaces left looking out to sea. Some fell completely, slithering to the sands in the night. Men would come from somewhere to examine the ruin, make notes and then go away again to be replaced by other men who would set fire to the debris where it lay on the beach. If it was dark I would watch the fire, impossibly drawn by it and its reflection in the now-calm sea. Each time one of the cottages fell, anybody who might still be living in any of the other cottages would walk to the scene in the airy post-storm breezes to contemplatively measure with their eyes the distance between the new cliff edge and their properties. Father had a fresh obsession: erosion.

He began to spend whole days shoring up the bit of cliff in front of our cottage with rocks and timbers which he bedded in the clay, making them stick out like lances against the tide. And of course the high water laid all his silly work to waste in a single hour.

He grew fearful of the sea and its pernicious ways, pacing the cottage, cursing softly, clenching his fists at each boom of the storm outside. He took to bringing drink back from the town, hitching a lift or carrying the stuff however many miles it was along the cliff top path. I became accustomed to watching him sleeping all hours of the day and night. While my own senses were being troubled by the ceaseless hiss of the ocean, I might hear him mumbling, coughing, calling to someone who was not there. Then at other times he might prepare an elaborate breakfast for the two of us, singing happily, enthusing over his plans for the day, brimming with nostalgia for things I did not believe had ever happened. I had learned enough about his moods, though I might savor them for their welcome lightness. He, like myself, grew thin and ghostly. Though it seemed we had weathered the worst of the winter, his exertions of both mind and body, his solitude, my liability to him, all seemed to have taken part of his health away and even his vast imagination began to fail to sustain him the way it had before.

In the back garden of the cottage I was mooching around one day when I caught and dislodged a stone with my foot. Underneath was a toad. It was biggish, old-looking, the ocher of the ground. Its presence surprised me. I thought it must be dead. I nudged it with my foot and it turned to face me. I debated over whether or not I should kill it. I ought to, I seem to remember thinking. The act of destroying a living creature might have done me good in some way, have transmuted something, imparted some kind of power, reinforced me. But I had never committed such an act and my will was now in decline. Carefully, my head spinning with just the small effort of bending down, I replaced the stone over the toad.

I began taking more and more to my bed, lying there still as the depths of the sea, slowing my breath until my ribs ached. The process at work within me was slowly gaining the upper hand. Somehow I was beginning to see my withdrawal from life as a way of lifting myself above time, transcending the conflict around me, holding at bay the demon that had come for my father and might soon come for me. I would doze in some twilight state that was neither sleep nor waking. I felt no hunger. Then sometimes I would find myself half-dressed in a corner of the cottage, alarmed at the fact that I could not recall getting out of bed and could not understand why I had gone there. Now and again I might venture out into the air and light to pick up bits of firewood or I might lift the stone in the garden to look at the toad, that unmoving, unblinking, ugly thing that drew me to it with an eerie, silent insistence. The thought of destroying it had long left my mind, indeed, I dared not touch it, not even with my foot. Then, after a while, I could no longer bring myself even to lift the stone.

On a gloomy, wet day my father and I were roused from our sleep by a polite knock at the door. At first neither of us could quite believe there might really be someone there. Then the knock became hard, and I could hear footsteps crunching through the undergrowth beneath my window. A helmeted head appeared. A gloved hand wiped the sandy film from the glass and the man's face peered down at me. I was so shocked I stood immediately and, clutching a sheet around me, went to fetch Father.

He greeted the man at the back door, complimenting him on what he said was a fine motorcycle. Apparently my father knew this man, someone from the place where we had lived before.

The man came into the kitchen and put his helmet on the kitchen table, his riding clothes smelling odd, his presence in our midst at once unsettling and inviting. He was bringing news, he said seriously. It was his sad duty, he felt obliged. Mother was dead.

▪ SIXTEEN ▪

THE MAN'S FEW words danced on the air between us, an earthly, factual statement that threatened to wake us from our dream, invite us to coalesce. Father became excitable, pressing the man for details. "Are you sure the boy should be listening to this?" said the man. "I mean, will he be able to understand?" "Yes," said my father. "Yes of course. He'll be all right. Come on, tell me what's happened." The man would no doubt have preferred his reticence, letting us find out from someone more qualified to speak, another member of the family perhaps, but it seemed he was familiar with us and knew how alienated and odd we were.

Naturally I was never told the full story; people, including this man, were either being kind or simply did not think to tell me. My mother, apparently, had formed some kind of a relationship with a patient at the hospital where she was staying. He was a temperamental type; not in the way that Father was, for despite his unpredictability and waywardness Father was a most innocuous man. This man was actively strange. One morning both he and my mother had declared themselves fit to leave the hospital and had jointly demanded their discharges. How well I came to know this type of man, how I ache when I think of him, his febrility, his plausibility, the tantrums; and I never did meet him.

They were given a room in a hostel somewhere and within a day or two arguments and fights began. I could picture my mother and her poor efforts at tidiness and cleanliness in this room, this place she could never have seen as her home. The man, unusually perhaps for his type, became psychotically jealous and began trailing Mother wherever she went, accusing her of being a whore, a thief, a man-hater out to cheat him of an inheritance that did not exist. He took offense at trivial things. He began to find evidence of my mother's supposed infidelity and dishonesty in the most curious of ways: the way milk bottles were arranged on a doorstep, in hairs on the landing carpet, the order in which she put on her clothes in the morning. She must have seen something in him, though. I fancied she saw it as some last chance in her life, compensation of sorts for what was obviously—even I could see it—a failed, scabby marriage and motherhood. Pride maybe, or resignation, must have stopped her leaving this madman, for she must have realized what he was like, or rather what he was not like. She herself was not mad, not in the proper sense of the word. She just gave in I think. I could picture her wearied at last and for always, her jaded hopes wresting what strength remained in her thin muscles as she lay back wherever it was and the man vented his terrific, incongruous fury on her, his hands around her neck, shaking, squeezing, and she offering not the slightest resistance, even smiling a little. Perhaps.

The man on the motorbike, having given only the most miserly of intimations about the details surrounding the affair, made some conciliatory gesture of condolence and left. My father sat opposite me in silence, unable to summon up the caricature of himself that passed for his personality. Then he stood and in an astonishing moment raised his hand to hit me across my head. He rocked with his own incredulity, the hard fist wavering above his temple as if it held something intolerably heavy. Eventually he let it fall and ran from the kitchen to the outside, turning over his chair and slamming the door hard as he went. I did not see him then for several days.

When he did return it was a wet and humid day. He cheerfully found some reasonable clothes for me, including an overcoat which I had long ago outgrown. He seemed more his usual self as he led me by the hand out of the cottage and along the cliff top to a café where we waited for a bus. We were going to my mother's funeral he told me.

A few people were at the church, relatives I assumed, but my father and I did not go inside. Something to do with not being a party to hypocrisy, I seem to remember him saying. We went on to the crematorium and I saw Alison looking distressed, trying vainly to hide her tears. I watched the coffin disappear through some swing doors and wondered what I was meant to feel. Afterwards we went to a little tea given by my mother's sister whom I did know, she having been to our old house lots of times when I was younger. Alison, looking composed and refreshed, sought me out as soon as she could. "You look awful," she said. "Are you eating properly? I bet you're not. I bet he hardly bothers with you. And I don't believe what he's telling everyone, about the school and all. You're not really going to school, are you, Peter?" "Of course he is," said Father, hurriedly interrupting. "He's top of the class in most things. Isn't that right, Peter?" Alison sighed and held my hand. Soon Father became drunk and started insulting everyone, dragging up old arguments and grievances, and we had to leave. Alison said she would try and fix something up for me to come and live with her, she would come and visit me as soon as she possibly could. But she never did and I do not recall ever having seen her in the years that were to follow.

We tramped through the wet night hitching lifts since my father had been unsuccessful in trying to beg money for our bus fares back to the cottage. He seemed very tired and he kept stumbling and found it difficult to get to his feet again. When we did get back he went straight to his bedroom. I heard the bed creak and then nothing. I lay on the sofa in my tight overcoat and looked at the cracks and swirls in the ceiling.

After a day or so, when he had not stirred from his room, I took it on myself to go and see if he was all right. I opened the door and approached his sleeping figure with my customary hesitancy and stealth. Only his head and bare shoulders were visible above the sweat-damp old blanket. His forehead, and beyond the hairline, was puffed in a series of bumps and ridges latticed with a spidery network of surfaced capillaries. The skin about his temples and cheekbones was similarly bloated, making his eyes small, like a pig's, or a small child's. He grimaced in his sleep, horribly so, his dry white lips parting to reveal sepia, scummed teeth. I crept round to the window side of his bed and saw his shoulders and the top of his back. The flesh was wet and convoluted like a brain, red sores running in lines between the contours. I couldn't help myself, I don't know why, and I was already reaching out to touch, to feel the texture and depth of his soft masses when he turned around, staring at me with his pinpoint black eyes. I snatched back my hand. With great difficulty he spoke: "I'm sick. It's real this time. You must help me, Peter. Try to understand."

I could not understand. In my hopeless confusion I ran into the kitchen and returned with a large knife. I held it over him. Already he had fallen asleep again. My hand was tight around the handle, grasping, sweaty. What was I meant to do? Then the knife was gone, falling away from me, slowly tumbling away from me, spinning, flashing, cutting my father's shallow breath and slipping harmlessly to the floor. I could no longer bear to look at him. I left the room closing the door behind me.

I wandered aimlessly about the rest of the cottage, my head spinning with too many thoughts. I went into the kitchen and gorged myself with whatever I could lay my hands on, old meat from the unused refrigerator, packeted cakes, bread, sweets, and more. Then I ran out of the cottage, through the garden and back to the cliff edge down which I scrambled to the beach. I began running again, the shale and coarse sand spraying from my feet, out to the edge of the tide, then back, under the dead gaze of the empty shops. There were a few people about, in pairs, with dogs, but nobody seemed to find anything unusual in a boy galloping to exhaustion along the cold wet beach, and no one sought to stop me as I gangled and stumbled, though eventually fatigue got the upper hand and I dropped to the ground, cuddling a piece of clay, my head filled with the red of weariness and misery. I felt the cold moisture of the clay against my cheek and the flames of tears in my eyes.

I rested for a while, then began the long walk back to the cottage. Where else was there for me to go? My lungs glowed inside me and I thought I recognized the first symptoms of a cold, though it was probably only the result of my unusual exertion.

The dark blue palms of night were growing and spreading from the inland horizon as I dragged myself back up the cliff and walked into the garden of the cottage. Something stirred near my foot, small, frightened, quickly gone, since, strain my eyes as I might I could not spot it in the gloom. The toad, no doubt, on one of its nightly forays—though I had never seen it anywhere but under the stone.

I went inside and closed the door gently behind me. The cottage was in darkness and I stood there for a long time, completely unsure of myself. Eventually I fumbled for the kitchen light and made my way across to the hallway to switch on the light there. I stood before the door of my father's bedroom, transfixed by some external message that had not yet permeated into my conscious mind. Then I realized what it was: the smell. Suddenly it overwhelmed me, the vomit, the stink of shit, and a quick throb in my temples sent me doubling over to throw up on the floor, buckets and buckets of the stuff.

I feel sure that my intention had been to find out how I could help him, but that may be a convenient trick of my conscience, a rationalization to make me feel more comfortable and less responsible. But if I had intended to offer him my assistance, that resolve vanished in an instant and I made my way to my own bed to sink into a sleep deeper than I had ever remembered or would ever know again.

. S E V E N T E E N .

HOW TOUGH A body is. How hard it is to make it relent, against its wishes. I cannot say how long I lay there, many days certainly, weeks maybe, listening, at first, to my father's low groans and mumblings, forcing myself not to hear by concentrating on the sound of the sea or the falling rain—ancient, accommodating sounds. At some point I began to be beleaguered by dreary hallucinations of cumuli of color before my eyes, armies of insects coming for me, that sort of thing. But they would pass and I would realize that the process was far from complete. My tongue became cemented into the roof of my mouth with the crud and residue of my seldom breath. My eyelids began to grate like paper and there was no comfort in keeping them either open or closed. I felt odd stabs of pain in my limbs, my stomach and heart. Then there were other times when I would be listening to the wind at its height, absorbing it, feeling myself rise above the thin outline of my body, rolling away from it, sharing with delight the wind's violence on our home and the earth, making an ally of it, a universal companion, trusting it the way I would trust a cancer, if I had one.

There would always be someone, though, it seemed, somebody trying to "save" me. A man came saying, "Forgive me, I'm looking for someone. Perhaps he is your father."

He was standing in the doorway to my room, his feet crunching broken glass the origin of which I did not know. He was dressed in a dark overcoat, and he carried a small brown case. Resentful of the intrusion I slipped momentarily back into my trance, then I looked again, turning my head this time. But the method I had chosen to abstract myself from the world was not sufficient, and I knew it; just turning my head had given the game away. The man came closer, tightly clutching his case as if for safety. "I am sorry," he said. "I'm from the National Insurance, you see. I say, are you all right? No," he said, a twitter of fear in his voice. "I can see you clearly are not all right. I shall get help."

He backed off, then mistakenly entered my father's room. A sledgehammer of stench rolled out of the room, the smell of bad meat, together with a black bubble of hissing flies. I heard the man's little gasps of dismay then saw him as he reemerged, a handkerchief cupped over his mouth and nose. He took a step into my room, his eyes looking at me over the hankie, pale, serious eyes; then he hurried off, clutching his case.

I remember a doctor standing over me, testing the reflexes in my elbows and ankles. He listened to my slow heartbeat, wiped the scum from my lips with a sweet-smelling damp cloth, then said I would live. Behind him, in my father's room, I heard the curses and quiet disagreements of the paper-masked men who had come to move my father's corpse. For some reason they could not agree on a particular way of doing something, some task, I didn't know what. I heard the rustle of sheets of plastic. The doctor pushed my bedroom door to. He tried opening a window but was unsuccessful. He made a great show of looking at his watch. He said nothing.

Eventually I too was moved, somewhere, I will never know where since the exertion I had felt during even the slight action of having my body picked up made me fall asleep before they had taken me from the cottage.

I was nursed back to consciousness, encouraged to drink, and eventually to eat again, by a kindly, ringlet-haired young man with a small face and sharp, pointed features. I was in a room of my own which was decorated with red rabbits and cartoon bears. Indeed they had me in some kind of cot where

I would lie most of the day, listening to the sounds of other children, probably much younger than myself, playing nearby, outside somewhere. The young man, he wore no kind of uniform, would come and praise me if I had eaten well. He would get me to sit out in a chair and by way of reward he would read stories to me from a book of one thousand and one such stories. What a freshness these stories imparted to me, a lightness, a release such as I had never known before. They radiated and lifted me from my preoccupations with myself. Sometimes he would show me pictures to please me, the sort of thing my mother, that dark stranger in my soul, might have done. I saw only one other person, a white-coated woman who dropped in on me on odd mornings, smiling, asking how I felt. I, of course said nothing. I should have known enough to be wary of this woman, not to have trusted her, but my wilfulness would lead me where it would.

I was taken from this place to some kind of home, a big house set back from a road, hidden behind tall trees, which looked out towards a straight blue horizon that was the sea, that awful, sucking expanse.

I was put in a dormitory with other boys. It was a crowded place. Many of the boys were very rough and when they could they would stand around me screwing their fingers in their temples, calling me weird and loony. And, as was the way of things, I was beaten up once or twice, though I felt they got little pleasure from this since I was never inclined to retaliate. The pain of these beatings was negligible: I seemed to be rising above pain in a curious sort of way. I was put in a classroom during the day, at a desk at the back of the class, though I never wrote anything or understood what the teacher was talking about. The teacher feigned understanding and patience with me, though I sensed his exasperation. The summer heat was intense and I fainted once or twice, since I was far from strong despite everyone's efforts. One day, without a thought in my head, I set off walking down the drive and out of the grounds. I walked straight across fields of deep green corn which rippled in the wind, waved and tressed like fantastic hair. I came to a road that looked familiar, though how I would have known it I could not imagine. I followed it down a rift in the hot landscape till I found the lure that had drawn me: the sea, the beckoning giant in my imagination and my nightmares. I walked on to the beach. There must have been something odd about my appearance because children stopped their playing and fell quiet as I passed. I just kept going, no reason, on and on for I don't know how long, under the shadow of the cliff. Then I came to a familiar place.

All the cottages had gone, and the shops, though they did not appear to have been claimed by the sea. The whole site was flat like a desert, the horizon broken only by a bulldozer and some kind of hut or mobile home. I climbed the cliff, careless of the loose clay beneath my feet, sometimes tumbling back down but then simply retracing my steps till I reached the top. I wandered about, inexplicably seeking the foundations of the cottage that we had lived in but there was not much to be seen save a few sharp, salt-edged weeds pushing up through a mazy piece of concrete. The heat began to draw my blood and I fell to the ground, the low sun burning on the top of my head. From the dazzle a small girl appeared. "Are you all right?" she asked. I raised my head a little. She kicked at the fine sand round her feet. "Have you seen what I've got?" she asked. And she lifted a stick up in the air from which a big old toad was suspended, its head and legs bound with a thin, cutting wire. It was alive, though very still: any movement would surely have been an agony for it, or perhaps have augured its death. It did not even blink. I dragged myself to my feet and made a weak gesture of pushing the girl away. She moved back a pace looking as if she was about to cry. Then she ran away, the old toad jangling on the end of the stick. I slithered back down to the beach, catching my head many times. The screams of the seagulls rose abruptly in my head, their wings beating in my chest. I lost my sight for a while, blackness encapsulated in terrific heat. And then I hoped I would die and be taken by the tide.

But it was not to be.

Slow footsteps came into the light shadows of my recovering vision. "We've been looking for you, sonny," said a voice. "Come on now, stand up. Gently does it." But his helping hands had to take all my weight. I could not move, had no strength, no desire to. Nothing was left in me at all. He laid me back on the hot sand and I reflected on the first wave of a warm, comforting stillness breaking over me, a quiet madness of my own making. In a funny sort of way it was how I imagined a homecoming might be. "Easy now boy," said the man. "You rest and I'll be back shortly."

I watched his dark legs scurry away, my sight having returned fully by this time, and allowed myself one last act, one last indulgence before the years that followed: I smiled.

·   E I G H T E E N   ·

THE MAJOR THUDDED the spade into the hard ground, lifting a heavy clod that rolled off before he could turn it and dig it back in. He threw the spade down and picked it up again. He cursed quietly under his breath, then scythed the blade through the tough carpet of weeds, drawing up a thin, shapely piece of turf. We were alone. All the other residents were supposed to have joined us in this task of converting an area of open woodland into some sort of vegetable patch, but the sudden and unexpected late frost, together with the rule that they were not obliged to take part in any ostensibly therapeutic work unwillingly, meant that everyone else had opted to stay at the house where they would suffer the discomfort of John and Anna's disapproving, indulgent looks in exchange for keeping agreeably warm. Neither the Director of One World nor his assistant could really have expected any of them to turn out in this cold, and it must have been a surprise when the Major openly challenged the house on their behalf, saying after breakfast, "If none of you will come with me then I shall start the job alone. And for company I shall take my friend Peter, since I know that if he could speak then he would wish to come." And for this outburst John and Anna were obliged to offer some vague support.

Though the Major had made a big show of dressing me carefully in overcoat, scarf, gloves and oversized hat, placing a blanket over my knees for extra warmth, it was not enough to keep out that grasping chill, that static coldness where ribbons of mist, like spectral mirages of the land beneath, twisted and grew substantial as the morning passed.

I was no longer quite myself, not up there in my head nor in that bony thin house they insisted was my body, the residing place of whatever they believed I really was, a soul, a vampire, a trickster perhaps. I had not been quite myself since those hours, that day, however long it was, when I had been subjected to the acrimonious details of my past, my history, whatever it may be called. Perhaps I had really seen nothing, an embellishment of nothing, and found it simply appropriate to explain myself with these excuses, these images, these baubles cast against the sky. I don't know what was true, have no idea of the nature of "truth." Those things in my mind—I couldn't trust them, not things like that so neatly arranged, two-dimensional, obvious to the point of being only declarable as null and void. That past I saw, if it was really mine, was not a past in which I could place any trust—it would only let me down, I know it would. To forget, if at all possible, that would be best.

John and Anna had come for me, points of light visible through the weave of the hood. Their feet, his shuffling, hers clicking, tripped about the cellar floor. One of them turned the creaky apparatus and I flipped over, my back coming to rest in an atrocity of pain. My limbs were freed but would not resume their customary positions unless manipulated. This seemed to bring sighs from them both. I might have hoped to be left for a while but they were eager to have me away up the wooden steps. My main joints grated, felt hammered as they lifted me up, up to the electric light in the hall of the One World Rehabilitation Center. They did not pause to rest, carrying on up the stairs to my room where I was put on the bed. Anna tugged at the ties of the hood still in position on my head. To my surprise I was quickly able to focus in the dull light. John bent over me, his breath damp and attractive. He probed at my chest with his stethoscope, moving it about impatiently, shaking his head. "Nothing," he said. "Just the same. I find it hard to believe. He's in there somewhere, the bugger, I know he is." He waved a finger, which Anna took as the signal to wrap a blanket roughly around me. He shrugged and they left, whereupon I fell immediately into a troubled sleep in which I dreamt they had made a deal with me whereby I would be allowed to remain passive while they amputated parts of my body and resurrected them independent of the main mass, promising to return them to my keeping at some later time.

When I eventually woke it was to find John alone in the room, sitting with one leg drawn up over the other. He looked rumpled and gloomy. He stood and went over to the sink to fetch a damp cloth which he wiped gently over my mouth. He picked a bit of loose skin from my lip with his thumbnail. "Now, my boy," he said, "how are you today?"

Under the darkness of his expression I saw an abiding flicker of excitement.

"I want you to tell me, Peter," he said, gagging on some kind of impatience, "how are you today?"

I saw a vein flicker in the corner of his jaw, a tiny manifestation of his apparent anger. "Come on," he said, "get up." He reached for me, his thick hands gripping my upper arms with an unusual strength. "Out of it, come on!" Some ghastly fluid lurched in my chest as he heaved me up, hugging me to him. He walked me around the room. "This is what we do, isn't it, Peter? We walk. Yes? And we talk to our fellow man. No one can exist like you; it just isn't humanly possible. There are no known cases. Come on, you bastard. Do it."

He squeezed me till I thought I would be sick. Round and round the small floor he dragged me, faster and faster, breaking into some sort of singing with the momentum: "Baby don't sleep, Baby don't cry, Spread your wings, Time to fly."

He threw me back on the bed and sank into the chair breathing very heavily, his head and shoulders rocking with the rhythm of his exhalations. He looked up at me as I lay across the bed, my arms spread wide. With some conscious effort he stopped breathing suddenly and began to laugh. "You old bugger," he said between lungsful of laughter.

"You crafty old sod. Why, the minute I get out of here you'll be jumping up from that bed, dancing, singing. Ah God, I don't know, I really don't. I take my hat off to you, Peter. They just don't come like you these days."

He composed himself, then came over to me and carefully lifted me onto the bed, properly, so that I was comfortable. "Look at me," he said in renewed humor. "Acting just like the others. Into bed, Peter. Want the wheelchair, Peter? I'll fetch you some lunch, Peter, your favorite today. Poor Peter. How sad."

He laughed drily, covered me with the blanket, then left the room.

My leg no longer flapped though I did still slobber when food was put before me. But this action was less marked and I felt that, given time, it too would no longer be a feature of my condition. Tom resumed the exercises with me one morning when it seemed to them that I had completed a vague stage of some sort of recovery. He had barely started rowing away with the machine when John came in, attracted no doubt by the sound, waved a finger and shook his head. Tom let me down from the apparatus and took me to the kitchen with him where he spent a happy, leisurely hour preparing lunch for the rest of the house.

The soft air of a false spring came to One World, whispering in the treetops and undergrowth around the house. Bits of green began to appear in the dark of the hedges round the small garden beyond the front drive. For much of the time I was left in peace in some corner of the house, though one afternoon the triplets became excited by a collective idea. They asked Tom if they could take me for a walk. He replied that he did not see why not. They took me out along the track that led to the house, then, when they were well out of sight of the place, quickly veered off through a gap in a thicket, pulling the chair over crackling ferns to a kind of den they had obviously made for themselves some time before. The most exotic of the trio posed before a piece of broken

96

mirror wedged into the crook of a low branch, pencilling make-up on her face, thick, heavy lines that made her features look grotesque. She poked a finger at her hair which was like that of the other two that day: held up by a yellow headband, wild and reaching like upturned roots. The other two were giggling in some preordained conspiracy, their arms locked together as they whispered. "I daren't," one of them said. "Go on, he won't do anything. He won't tell anyone, you know." One of them freed herself from her sister and came over to me. The exotic one paid no attention as the one who had been chosen fumbled with the buttons on my trousers, getting bolder as each second passed, till she had peeled back the material and unfolded the top of the incontinence pad. She screwed her lips up and was joined by the other interested party. "Touch it," she said, "go on. Get hold of it." The girl puzzled for a moment, then reached for my prick, sliding her cold hand underneath till it rested in her palm. "Hah," said the watching sister, as if on the verge of some important discovery. "Now you have to rub it," she said, "and make it stiff." The girl scratched vaguely and tentatively. "Not like that," said the watcher, "harder. Like this." But before she could get hold of me I pissed, the thick gold liquid shooting from me onto both sisters. The girl wrenched her hand away. "Uuugh, the dirty bastard," she said, shaking her hand, wiping it on the grass. The other sister flicked my trousers over my prick. The exotic one, who had begun to take an interest in her sisters' activity, sniffed and said, "Well if that's the only way you two can think of getting a man, I feel sorry for you. This face is my fortune." Then they began arguing and ran off into the woods chasing each other, their raucous voices trailing some distance away, further, till I could no longer hear them. Much later, when the light was failing, the exotic one came back for me, did up my fly quickly, then pulled me from the thicket and hurriedly pushed me back to the house without a word.

I was not quite myself during those days. My blood lay

heavy like mercury inside me, surging at times, making me weary and feverish. Then the wintry weather returned with some kind of vengeance, a retaliation against everyone who had forgotten it.

· N I N E T E E N ·

OFTEN I WOULD be left in the hall, looking out of the window at the snows falling and suddenly melting in the quick warmth of the suppressed spring. Everyone went about their business in a cool, lethargic way, suggesting some kind of hiatus, a waiting for something I could not quite understand. It mattered little to me, of course—they would do with me what they would—but a dry fear would often drift through me that I might be left in this place for a long time yet, suffering John's resurgent enthusiasm and painful treatments. I could not have stood that.

But I need not have worried.

Some time on, when the weather had eased and at last brought a genuine promise of spring, I was hustled into the lounge by the Major. He seemed very rough and excited. "I know what they did to you," he said. "They got warned off about using that drug after the Kaufmann inquest. Bastards. Don't let them get to you, Peter, you're doing fine. Don't let them take you apart. Shouldn't be much longer now. I drafted a letter the other day. I'd read it to you if I could be sure this place wasn't bugged. Later, maybe. Come on, let's get out in God's fine weather. He's on our side, you know, God, good old egg that He is. Bugger me, I'm in a good mood. Haven't slept since I wrote that grand epistle. Out of it, let's go."

He pushed me along the path to the clearing. To my surprise I found virtually all of the other residents there—I had not seen them leave the house, but so much I could put down to my preposterous self-preoccupation. The Major left me beside a small hole, at the bottom of which was a dark puddle. He pushed a hoe into my hand. "Just for effect old man," he said, winking, his dirty face beaming under his spiked, wild hair.

The others were sitting around the big square of land rarely speaking, wishing, no doubt, that they had not been press-ganged into this labor which could hardly have suited such as the triplets, who had now become inseparable and sat on a log toying with each other's fingernails and hair. The Major rushed about the plot chivying everyone, talking about which type of crop might be suitable in which position, not caring if anyone objected, quickly acquiescing if anyone remarked on the futility of the exercise. But his overall demeanor would not be denied—he was sort of happy, excessively so; I knew, I had an eye for such things.

The sun rose high above us and the few that had actually started some kind of work became bored and distracted and began rolling cigarettes and wandering off into the woods. The Major was digging a hole and paid scant attention to their comings and goings. Then Tom arrived, lured from his kitchen by the warm air and the light in which he seemed to take great pleasure.

The Major welcomed the old man with a white-toothed smile and a handshake. Tom good-humoredly extended his own hand and the two sat on a pile of stones. They made a joke about using me as a scarecrow and seemed easy in each other's company. Tom brought a packet of cigarettes from his cardigan pocket and offered one to the Major, who declined, saying he preferred to roll his own. I realized that Tom was a little embarrassed to be seen in such comfortable company with the Major, though he disguised it well, returning the man's flippant comments with much tact and conviviality. Had I thought about it, I should not have thought the two had anything in common at all, but such is the way among odd people like us—we are thrown together in odd, explosive mixtures, and in the name of survival it seems that relationships must somehow be formed. The rest of the residents slowly reappeared from the woods, drawn, perhaps, by Tom's fibrous voice, wondering about being caught idle by this ancillary member of the house staff, unsure of the implications, uncertain as to whether or not they should start work again. Eventually they settled for playing a game, pitching stones into a circle drawn on a piece of barren earth. They were a poor lot, really. They had done nothing, even I could see that. Tom did not seem inclined to make a fuss, though, preferring a quiet conversation with the Major, ignoring the others save for an occasional glance in their direction. The Major stood and paced the weed-strewn ground, kicking at things, making an odd noise halfway between a cough and a laugh.

I saw him first. John. His brown, round outline wove through the undergrowth behind the slender fingers of a proliferation of birch trees. I wanted to push the hoe I was holding to the ground, to let it fall, warn the others somehow, since I was the only one, I felt, who saw something amiss in their behavior. But I could not help them, they—my friends? Sundry black clouds—I do not add this for effect—were coursing through the sky as he emerged into the patchy sunlight, striding across the coppice, coming quickly among us.

"So," he said, "this is how you abuse the trust I have placed in you, idling, wasting your time, and mine." The other residents continued with their game in a fit of acute embarrassment. "Tom," he said, "I am surprised. You of all people. Perhaps the time has come when we must reconsider your employment with us. Maybe you should be thinking about going back to the hospital. You have not quite been yourself lately, have you?"

Tom looked downcast. He rubbed the back of his neck and could not bear to look at the Director. The Major clicked stones in the palm of his hand while the others, one by one, stopped their game to listen to John.

"Here," John said. "All of you. You must listen to me. This concerns everyone connected with the One World Rehabilitation Center." He drew a piece of paper from the pocket of his dirty green jacket. "We have," he said, "one among us who seems to doubt the integrity of the service you are offered in our house, this place, this last hope in all your lives. Someone in our small company has taken it upon himself to complain, if it can be called a complaint, to the high authorities, the board responsible for the fiscal and moral provisions for One World. If a single word of these outrageous allegations were true, then I might offer praise for this man's initiative. But this—" he held up the paper at arm's length and quoted: *"They beat us up and shove us down in the cellar. If we are sick and cannot control ourselves then we are deprived of food. Privileges, such as free access to the toilets, are given meanly. They are out to break us, come what may. You know how many people die here, you must have it on record somewhere. If you haven't then I will supply the information. The people who run this place are tyrants. The poor souls in their care fear every waking moment that they too will be singled out for torture. They are sick, we all are. You've got to investigate."*

"Is this," John asked, "how you choose to repay our kindness? Our genius? You among us? Are you listening? Well, I have news for you. This morning I have been in a meeting with two representatives of the board and they will be back later to interview the rest of you. As for the author of this absurd piece of polemic and baseless accusation, I must inform him that they have looked scrupulously into his medical history and recommended that he be removed from the Center immediately to some more open place where his subversive activity can be scrutinized in detail."

He clattered spades, forks and trowels into a pile. "Right, everyone, back to the house. Come on. Move it." Tom dutifully made for me and had already released the brake on the chair when John interrupted, "Not him. He can stay here a while." The Major stepped forward, anger boiling in the dark veins under the dust on his face. "But why?" he said. "Why him? You've got something to answer for, you bastard." He lunged for John, but his clawing hands stopped inches short of their apparent quarry. The color fell from him and he dropped to the ground sobbing, his voice retching and ebbing. John looked down at him, a mildness settling his contorted expression, a shifty satisfaction glowing out of him. The others had already begun picking their way among the trees to the path that led back to the house. John stooped to help the Major back to his feet. "Stephen," he said softly, "don't take on so. We shall care for you. Somehow we'll repair the damage. Have faith in us. Trust us. We can make good again, can't we?" "Yes," said the Major, snuffling. "Yes, I think we can." "Good boy," said John. "Now away with you back to the house and we'll have a long chat about it all, eh?" "Yes," said the Major. "A long talk. I'd like that." He ran off to join the rest. Tom, who had been waiting at the edge of the clearing, took his arm and guided him away.

John supervised their disappearance, then turned to me. His eyes were on fire. "God, but you're a cunning bastard," he said. "If I were not a scientific man I would say you were the Devil himself. What chaos, what evil you must carry around in you. If I ever come across your case again I shall not be able to account for my actions. How do you do it? What demon's secret have you learned? Tell me. Tell me now, you bastard. Tell me!"

He grabbed at my clothing and lifted me from the chair. I felt the heat from his grimy face. He held me up in the air and shook me. Then he let me fall to the ground and walked away.

A long time passed. Pellets of water fell from the sky, followed by hail and a beating wind in this the last whiplash of a vengeful winter. Voices came to the trees, old voices, familiar, one of them perhaps my father's, telling me I should stand and fight the monster in this storm. But I could not believe it was him, could not interest myself in the mad spirits wheeling about in the crazy air around me. I was a child again. And I was old, older than I could ever have imagined. I saw myself lying prostrate across my own grave. I shall drown in this mud, I thought. And somehow, somehow it would be no more than I deserved.

■ T W E N T Y ■

I WAS BEFORE a face, a huge face etched in soft stone, seas of eye, a face that was the glum recipient of stories, thousands of stories, and I was a tiny thing in front of it, irritating its golden contours, a fly on a giant screen filled with its shine and impassivity. It breathed softly. It stifled a belch and retreated, twitching, some way off across the room, far enough to resume its normal proportions, its reassuring human design. A man. A man in a white coat. "Interesting," he said, addressing a colleague. "Read the history, it will stir your imagination. I have not seen the likes of this one before. He excites me, the romantic in me. How old would you say he is? Yes, I know. Difficult, isn't it? And Christ, isn't he thin? Can't be seventy pounds. Where would he find the strength to fight a sickness like this? You will, of course, have already diagnosed bronchopneumonia. The bilateral basal crepitations are very pronounced. On the dementia wards we call it the old man's friend. How long would you give a case like this? No voluntary movements? A ridiculous diet? Dehydrated? Thinner than a shadow? A still life in bone, hair, and awful flesh? What would you say? Come on. The relatives are at your throat, wanting to prepare for mourning. Twenty-four hours? Half a week? If you want me to answer seriously for you, I would say that this man should not now be alive. Whatever you say would be wrong. This is beyond medicine, if the history is to be believed. The soul is mentioned in no textbook, yet it is without doubt the most singularly influential factor in health, illness, dying, survival. Here we have a remarkable example of a soul, in there, somewhere in that rag doll of a man, a zest for life, a will to carry on. Look! Look at the blood results. Look here at the observations. Where does it come from? There is much to be learnt here, much for the philosophizing mind to get its teeth into. The articles we could write, the tests we could perform—surgery maybe, since I hear he has no family, no one to claim him. Perhaps not," he said with a smile and a sigh. He beckoned his friend to accompany him to the next bed.

Instruments tinkled on a tray somewhere nearby. I saw a tube running into my arm from a plastic bag filled with clear fluid. A female nurse drew back the curtain and came to my bedside. "Wakey, wakey, sleepy one," she said gently. She laid a tray on the locker next to my head. She shook a thermometer and slipped it under my arm, folding my hand across my naked chest. She smiled briefly as she took my pulse, then entered something on a chart she plucked from the end of the bed. From under a towel on the tray she produced a bowl full of something steamy. She began spooning the stuff up to my mouth but my lips would not part, my chin clamped up against the rest of my head. The hot liquid dribbled from the sides of my mouth, down my cheeks and into the hollows where my shoulders began. She poked a sharp fingernail into my mouth and tried to lever it open. Then she withdrew her finger and with it came a tooth and a little blood. She sat back and assumed a stern expression, dropping the tooth, with some distaste, in the tray. Behind her hard looks I sensed a small fear flickering and sparking for long enough to make her leave my bedside. When she came back she seemed to have recomposed herself. "All right, then," she said, "we'll try again." She offered the spoon once more, and the same happened. "If that's the way you want it then," she said. From somewhere she conjured a big syringe, drew liquid from the bowl and forced the beak of the instrument into the side of my mouth opposite to where she had found the tooth. The sweet fluid issued into my mouth, chafed at my throat, then disappeared inside me. "That's better," she said. "Now once more."

I could not say how long I had been in that place, that ordinary hospital peopled by normal cases with only physical sicknesses. I don't know where it was or how I had been brought there. I remembered little of my fate at the hands of the storm as it beat down on me in the open space in the woods. It may have been nothing more than a shower, I never was much of a judge of such things. I guessed it had been a long time ago, and that I had certainly slept for days, weeks maybe, though what had brought me back to life was as puzzling to me as it was to the doctor who had been treating me. And there was another question which dwelt briefly in my mind: Why had the Major signed my name at the bottom of his letter to the authorities? Of course I would never know, but then what did I really know about anything that went on in the minds of the people around me? Nothing.

I was never to return to the One World Rehabilitation Center and I was never to learn its fate or that of the people in it. No one ever thought to tell me.

This hospital was a good, careworn, happy place and I believe I should have been quite happy to spend what remained of my days hooked up to the plastic bag, waiting for whatever end Nature might have in store for me. But it was not to be. As soon as I was well enough, that is according to their standards, a psychiatrist was called to interview me. I, of course, said nothing. He quickly took the hint and the next thing I heard was him standing at the nurses' station ringing round various places trying to get me in somewhere.

I was loaded out one morning into an ambulance. The journey was short, and before the vehicle stopped I had a reasonable idea of my destination for out of the clear glass at the top of the windows I saw large, familiar black bricks, the flat red of a laundry building, trees whose outline was as intimate to me as the dry skin on my hands.

They stopped and opened the rear doors to lift me down under the glare of the Head Nurse. "Inside," he said.

▪ T W E N T Y · O N E ▪

MUCH HAD CHANGED on the Admission Ward during my absence. Tanya had gone, and many of the young men too, their places taken by others who had quickly acquired their predecessors' habits.

I was taken from the ambulance and wheeled straight through to the dormitory where, according to their quaint procedure of dehumanization, I was stripped and placed in night clothes which I would wear for the next seventy-two hours. This rule was imposed throughout, no matter what the nature of each case might be. My property, such as it was, was duly recorded and taken away somewhere, I don't know where. Then I was left beside a bed until the evening when I was summarily retrieved from the locked dormitory and taken through to the dining room. A large, familiar, syringe was produced. I was beset by a crushing depression, the reason for which I could not understand.

The following day Beckerminster came to where I sat in the dayroom. "How are you, Peter? How have they been looking after you these last few months? Cat still got your tongue?" he said with a chuckle. He put his hand on my shoulder. "Not to worry old man," he said. "Not to worry. You're safe here."

Perhaps the only remarkable thing about the day after my return was the fact that it coincided with the readmission of someone at first only vaguely familiar. They began by calling him Mr. Doultas, and then later, Roger. He was very agitated and looked difficult to control. He sat quietly for only a few minutes, then he began turning over tables and the young men came in force to take him away somewhere. He was, of course, the man who had occupied the bed next to mine on my previous stay in this place. He had survived, it seemed, though I do not think he was quite the same as he had been before he took the blade to himself. Part of his brain had gone with the heavy loss of blood, that was certain. His arrival both puzzled me and lifted my spirits. Beckerminster's friendliness and the nurses' residual detachment led me to the conclusion that I was not being held to blame for this man's attempted suicide—they were bearing no grudge and seemed to have quite forgotten the way my departure and his unobserved, self-inflicted harm had laid side by side, incidents on the same bad day. But then this was a busy place and many mad and bad things could happen in the space of a day.

My misery faded and I had new hopes that I might at last have found a permanent retreat. I accommodated myself quickly to my surroundings, compromising the way all human natures must compromise, telling myself it was not such a terrible place and I had known worse. But it was not to be.

Before the week was out Beckerminster came over to me again before his ward round—an action incredible in itself, since the Head Nurse insisted that all patients were seen by the doctor in the sanctum of his office, and all had to make themselves available during the ward rounds, which were always at the same time of day on the same day each week. However, the kindly doctor made this remarkable exception —the way he had done on my return—and came over to me. "Sorry old man," he said, "but I'm afraid you can't stay here."

He ambled over to the office to suffer the discontent of the Head Nurse, though I guess he might have dismissed him quite casually for he seemed a capable man.

His news came as no surprise to me, I had become so used to upheaval. I saw his words standing on the air in front of me, shimmering before they disappeared into their own negativeness. What else was I to do? I could offer no protest or thanks; I could only sit and wait until they came for me, wheeling me out into the dull afternoon and on to my last resting place.

TWENTY-TWO

I HAVE BEEN here . . . ah, but I do not count the years, have no talent for it, that much you must know about me by now. I am yet the youngest, I feel, though there is one not much older than myself. His name is Roger. He has followed me down the short path to this sad destination. No, I must correct myself, not sad, it would never do for me to call this a sad place.

I was brought from the Admission Ward across the square at the center of the hospital, past the laundry and Industrial Unit, to this ward which has a name, a woman's name, though I am constantly apt to forget what it is. Not to worry. They, all uniformed, allotted me a bed, a place at the dining table, and a chair in the dayroom, though they were soon to dispense with the effort of hauling me up to the table for my nutrition. And I waited days, many weeks, am perhaps still waiting, for word of some new home for me, some new treatment that someone anxious to make a name for himself feels might reverse what they see as my relentless decline. But no one speaks, no one comes, and I am here still, have been for . . . ah, if only I knew. If only it were important to know.

I am not as I was, not in any respect, least of all physically. My arms began crooking up during the nights and became eventually impossible for the nurses to hold down. The palms of my hands now face outwards at about shoulder height, my fingers wasting and spread, curling in, the nails growing and cutting my flesh if no one thinks to trim them. I am impossibly shaped. If it were possible to stretch me out they would see how much I had shrunk. My legs are now very thin, skeletal, drawn up and outwards. Soon my knees will reach my ears. And my insides? Souped; all the colors I had imagined the various parts to be must now surely be one simply gray mass, dried and brittle. My back has assumed a wetness, the flesh feels raised, and they dress it every now and again with a huge bandage. For this procedure they wear masks since the area apparently exudes a caustic smell they find unpalatable or perhaps dangerous. As a result of my awkward frame I am placed lengthways between the two arms of a reclining chair during the day to help keep my little weight off my burning sacrum. First they tried a rubber ring but this tended to irritate my badly nourished skin, so now they use a battery-powered rippling cushion on which I am seated and gently nudged by its hypnotic waves.

We are not taken out much, not at all, in fact, but this does not bother me: I would fear for myself these days if I were suddenly exposed to strong sunlight. And there are no daily trips from this place to the Industrial Unit, or anywhere else, since none of the clients here is capable of performing any more than the most animalistic of functions.

There are both men and women here and all, save Roger and myself, are quite ancient. They wander incessantly, the women more so than the men, trying locked doors, picking hopeless fights, though many are remarkably agile. The air is impregnated with the constant smell of feces and urine. Many talk constantly about their mothers, screaming for them sometimes, their voices seeming to come from crazed souls that have already passed on to the grave in advance of their crumbly old bodies.

In their wanderings many will pause in front of me and ask me questions, sometimes appearing quite rational and considerate: "You poor thing. Can nothing be done to help you? How awful for you." And this leads me to believe that my appearance has become shocking beyond the norm I had assumed before—even the demented old ladies see how bad I am. I should not let it concern me.

There are three large areas central to this ward—the sprawling dormitory, the dining room, and the dayroom. At each mealtime the wanderers are herded from dayroom to dining area, bawled at and pleaded with to stay in their allotted places, and served at lightning speed, since there seem to be no more than three nurses to the thirty or so of us at any time of the day. Some receive visitors who bring sweets, and flowers which are quickly removed after their visit since they may be eaten by one or two of the residents. The behavior of some of these normal people is often reserved, sometimes extraordinary, as they move about the ward stuffing chocolate into the residents' mouths, my own included, though this is always met with polite intervention when it is pointed out, wrongly, that I am prone to choking and am only to be fed under the supervision of qualified staff. At this many blush and retreat, and it would be interesting to note how many of them came back.

When it begins to get dark the noise becomes tumultuous and confusion is at its worst. The residents become hopelessly disorientated, unconsolably concerned about where they will spend the night, despite the fact that many of them have probably been in here for years. All will die here, that much I now understand.

Eventually most begin to tire and drop into the bright, plastic-covered chairs, unable to muster more than a jaded irritability. I look at their faces framed by the hard, gaudy chairs—pale, blank, like almonds on a mosaic.

Later still, all are roused and herded down to the dormitory, the big door being unlocked and swung open to reveal the large bays surrounded by unused curtains. I am taken first since I require the most effort to change—though now they bother little about putting me in pajamas and settle for simply draping the top about my shoulders to impress some invisible supervisor I have never seen. There is another reason for my being taken first, simply that I will not fall out of bed as some of the others are prone to do. Some of the beds—usually no more than two or three, sometimes none at all—are occupied by the dying, their rapid, shallow, rattling breaths being quickly drowned by the tramp of slippered feet from the dayroom. I sleep little, if at all, and never after the nurses' round in the early hours of the morning when they come and peel back the covers on everyone's beds, the various foul perfumes rising in one malodorous miasma with their soap and steaming water, a whiff from my own minuscule offering joining it all as it hangs in the air then is gone, up to the high ceiling, filming on the floor, who knows where? Then the light comes, that quietest of moments punctuated only by the nurses' giggles and whispers and the occasional screech of a peacock in the hospital grounds—my blood is no longer stirred by this sound.

Ah, this place, this huge, solid place. What mind, what hands designed it? These stone arches and pillars thicker than a man's length, the bolted metal window frames, the great wide doors that slam like bombs, the awesome weight of this place, holding me in its shiny-white proper angles, a tiny thing now, a little piece of meat cradled in a hard shell—who, what philosophy, what science caused such a monstrous construction? Its space, its honeycombed heavy structure, all that I know of it, have known of it, leaves me quite giddy, excited and yet serene, and I am happy if I dare to think that it is now in the process of absorbing me for all eternity.

I F I D R E A M these days it is with my eyes open, the images in my head no longer sliding on, oblivious of, unreal and unrelated to, the hard things in front of my eyes, the crazy ones brushing against my feet and the back of my head, the hands that cradle me from chair to bed.

I remember quite recently dreaming once again of my death, the manner of which I fail to recall—a simple fading away, perhaps? It would seem appropriate that way. A large mouth drew me upwards, pulling me with its mighty breath. This and other things I saw imposed on my mind while in front of my eyes the quivering activity went on, regardless of me and my madness.

Often I wish I were ill, genuinely sick. That way I could justify my meanderings and ramblings, negate them somehow, cast them outside of myself, become innocent.

ONE DAY, YESTERDAY, a month ago, I don't know, in another dream perhaps, one of the staff came to me. She looked down at me, opened her mouth, then seemed to think it more suitable if she knelt down to my level. She appeared different from the person I had always taken her to be—hard-voiced, authoritarian—and her words were carefully chosen and polite, seeming to come from a distance away, deep inside her.

"Peter," she said, "you have a visitor."

The chair across which I was spread was carefully trundled through to a quiet little room with plain cream walls and a high window.

It would, of course, be a terrible mistake, the sort of thing for which I had been made painfully accountable so many times in the past. A comb was passed through what remained of the hair on my sore, wet scalp. The nurse's fingernail picked something scabbed from the corner of my eye. Then the visitor was brought.

A chair was hustled in behind this small, straw-haired, murky-complexioned woman. The door of the room was locked behind her.

"Peter," she said. "Do you remember me? I am Alison, your sister."

A trick, had to be. What awesome lengths they would go to in these places. Once more I was being pursued. Again I had allowed myself to fall asleep, become complacent, overconfident about the security of my surroundings and the possibilities of my being able at last to rest.

The woman, whoever she really was, began telling me about herself. I noticed how genuinely embarrassed she was to start with, then how quickly she seemed to warm, become comfortable in my presence, realizing, no doubt, as others inevitably did, that I posed no kind of threat.

She told me how long she had been searching for me, how many times in her life she had asked herself if I could possibly still be alive. Clever stuff, and no mistake. She showed me photographs she said were of her son, I forget the name she used. She leaned awkwardly forward and placed them close to my nose. She'd got married once, she said, adding, "Can you believe it? Me? Married?" This amused her for a moment, I don't know why. Then she said that it had not worked out, was doomed from the start or something. She went quiet for a while, looking back over her shoulder to see, I imagine, if the nurses were standing there eavesdropping on her monologue. Then she went on.

It was a long time, she said, before she had been told about Father's death. She had demanded information about me instantly, she said, but by that time I had been moved about so much that no one really knew where to start searching for me. This she blamed on the aunt who had looked after her, who had always hated our father and for some reason had decided to take equal exception to me. "But please, Peter," she said, "you must never hold it against her, she was very good to me, saw I went to the right school, worked hard. She died last year. That's when I first had the idea of doing something about trying to find you."

I was becoming insidiously impressed. No one had ever recounted these details of my past life before, these baubles now formed into words, pouring innocent and enticing from the mouth of this pretty woman. Could it be possible? Might she really be Alison? My blood raced, lightly though, making me feel buoyant, fragile, new, newer than I had ever known.

"Do you remember the cottage?" she asked smiling. "That awful place at the coast? The sea? Those dreadful storms at night? Oh God, Peter," she said with a giggle, "and do you remember that time we cremated a dead cat? Weren't we terrible? I mean, weren't we just a dreadful pair? Still," she said, sighing, "I suppose we meant well."

Then she seemed to run out of words and her face became still and firm. She stood and leaned with her back against the wall, pacing the few steps across the room then stopping again to examine me minutely, her now impassive eyes absorbing my obscene shape, my ugly, withered face and my bad, slithery skin. Then she fell to the floor in front of me and took hold of the brittle claw that passed for my hand.

"Oh, you poor thing," she said plaintively, "you poor, poor soul. What has happened to you? What is it that's eaten you away like this? Such a waste, such a dreadful, awful waste."

Her face was close to mine. I saw my reflection in her big eyes. Then she let go of my hand and stood, smoothing her skirt. She picked her bag up from the floor, neatly placed the chair to one side, then knocked on the window in the door. The nurse who had let her in came and bounced her key in the lock. "Well?" she asked.

"It's not him," said the woman. "He may well be called Peter, but I'm afraid that is not my brother. I am sorry to have bothered you."

"Oh, not to worry," said the nurse. "I'll show you the way out, shall I?"

"Yes, thank you," said the woman.

She turned in the doorway.

"Isn't it sad," she said looking back at me. "Can't anything be done for the poor creature? Anything at all?"

"I'm afraid not," said the nurse.

The woman, Alison, my sister, sighed.

"Good-bye Peter," she said.

I LOSE TRACK of the seasons. There seems no point in trying to pin them down. Once I must have thought it worthwhile from the point of view of my own comfort perhaps, but now it seems a quite futile exercise. Every day seems just the same as the last one, my limbs, all parts of me, becoming more wasted or shrunken. And my sight, periodically, seems to be failing. The moving shapes in front of me become dark, formless, colorless and hazy, hissing, if that's the way I can describe a shape. Sometimes, if there is a sudden, sharp noise —say, a window being broken by one of the patients, or an unusually high-pitched scream—then my sight becomes clear momentarily, though it is never for long. I confess that I no longer care much about my sight. I no longer care about anything I suppose. The day will come, my last day, and I sense it is not far away, not far away at all . . .

FOR A WHILE they seem to have been concerned about me. I can no longer tolerate food or fluid, I don't know why. It's certainly through no conscious effort on my part, for I have always accepted whatever was offered me since the very first day I was brought here. Somehow I can no longer take the stuff into my system. It could be that my tubes and innards have become so dry and congealed that nothing will enter in or pass out. Or it could be that my body has simply given up the ghost; it cannot go on forever, I know that.

The nurses bend over me, shrug their shoulders, and quietly, reverently, remark how I have done well to have lasted so long. Today, this day, they have decided to leave me in bed.

A man in a white coat is brought to offer an opinion. He puts his ear against my naked chest, his nose between my parched lips, then he retreats, shaking his head. "Fascinating," he says. "Absolutely fascinating. Never seen the like before. It's as if," he says, "he's in some kind of suspended animation, or hibernating perhaps. God knows what we do in a situation like this. Bring me the notes," he says.

He reads my history, that decaying sheaf of papers and notes I once drooled over but could not now care less about.

"Can't be too careful in a case like this," he says. "The poor man. We must do our best by him. Occasions like this," he ingenuously remarks, "require the very best we can offer by way of our imagination, our compassion. We've had our eyes on him for some time, I must admit. And don't we need the bed? Look at him, isn't he in an awful state? He's in there, though, we're certain of it. He's there all right, dreaming, thinking, watching us with some terrible, secret eye."

He comes closer, kneels at the bedside.

"Are you there, my friend? Can we help?"

An age passes. I see whole continents in his pink skin, worlds and constellations in the features of his face. Then, though he makes not the slightest movement, he becomes distracted, himself again.

"We shall give you something," he says. "Something, Peter, to make quick and light of your suffering."

He is unrecognizable now, crazed with his idea. He beckons the nurse away with him. They talk quietly, conspiratorially. I can yet imagine, still infer, some easy, diplomatic agreement. They leave and I wonder at the failing of day and light, at the night which is about somewhere, outside, its weight pressing on the roof of the building, pressing on me. I vaguely discern the cleaving of the darkness by the lights of the vehicles that pass beneath the dormitory windows. I dream of the awful sea I once knew, of cold wind in the treetops. I am afloat. Their hands reach for me, fix me with wire, suspend me, no, pull me down into a hollow in the damp earth. I hear the sound of a heavy stone being pulled along the ground. I hear their grunts, I know much of their burden and weariness. They moan about the effort of manipulating the stone until it is in position over me, hard on my back, excluding the light, though I, stiff Peter, Peter the toad, can yet hear the mindless wind at work somewhere, above, below, inside me, I don't know where . . .

I wake. The dormitory lights are on. Tough footsteps get louder, encircle me. I see the two girls, these sweet, rude angels, and their trundling, white, metal box whose lid they lift to produce a dish tinkling with glass and metal jewelry. Reverently, they draw back the covers that hide me. An afterthought, a little laughter: they pull the curtains that surround the bed. And now, impassively, they toy with their brilliant bits and pieces: a syringe, a needle, a phial or two. I wonder at the extraordinary care they use in preparing for their procedure: thick gloves, checking and counterchecking. Their mixture is precious, I see that. Not to be fooled around with.

I contemplate my last moments and wait for the explanation I know will not be offered.

BOOK MARK

The text of this book was set in the typeface
Garamond by Berryville Graphics, Berryville, Virginia.

The display was set in Gill Sans and Gill Sans Ultra
by Maxwell Typographers, New York, New York.

It was printed on 50lb Glatfelter, an acid-free paper
and bound by Berryville Graphics, Berryville, Virginia.

Designed by Ann Gold